THE
TELLTALE TURKEY
CAPER

THE TELLTALE TURKEY CAPER

•

Book Five
in
The Jennifer Gray Veterinarian Mystery Series

•

GEORGETTE LIVINGSTON

AVALON BOOKS
THOMAS BOUREGY AND COMPANY, INC.
401 LAFAYETTE STREET
NEW YORK, NEW YORK 10003

PRINTED IN THE UNITED STATES OF AMERICA
ON ACID-FREE PAPER
BY HADDON CRAFTSMEN, SCRANTON, PENNSYLVANIA

For Mike and Melody Jean,
with love and appreciation.

Chapter One

Wondering which was worse, to be awakened on Thanksgiving morning by a jangling alarm clock after only a few hours' sleep, or hearing the worst storm of the season battering the house, Jennifer Gray resisted the urge to burrow under the covers. She turned on the Tiffany lamp beside her bed, and her pale pink bedroom was filled with soft warm light. It was a start. Maybe if she could get her feet on the floor, and splash a little cold water on her face . . .

"Will you please tell me how I'm supposed to take a shower with a turkey in the tub?"

"If I don't get that blasted turkey de-

1

frosted, *nobody* is going to have Thanksgiving dinner!"

Jennifer stuffed her feet into fluffy white slippers, and groaned. It wasn't unusual for her grandfather and Emma to be bickering about something. It had become a way of life over the years, and most of the time they enjoyed their energetic debates. But at six o'clock in the morning?

Wes grumbled something, and Emma returned, "It has to be defrosted under cold running water, or it takes days in the refrigerator, Mr. Wes, and you and I both know I don't have days, only hours. There is no way I can fit a twenty-pound bird in that newfangled double sink you insisted on putting in the kitchen! And if you *really* want to blame somebody, call the butcher! I ordered a twenty-pound *fresh* turkey, not that thing in the bathtub!"

"What's wrong with using the washtub in the laundry room?" Wes asked dejectedly.

"It's full of cut flowers, and you have no idea what I went through to get them! Annie at the florist shop finally had to special order them all the way from Omaha, and if that wasn't enough, the orders got mixed up. I wanted orange and yellow chrysanthemums and ended up with white and yellow. And until I can round up all the vases . . ."

"What about the sink in the church kitchen?"

"You expect me to carry a twenty-pound turkey all that way?"

"It's not that far," Wes reminded her. "But no, I don't expect you to carry it. I'll take it over."

"Have you looked outside? We're in the middle of the worst storm of the season. Do you want to catch pneumonia?"

"I know it's nasty out there, Emma. That's why I'm not out on my morning jog to the river."

"Okay, you two," Jennifer said, joining them in the hallway. "It's Thanksgiving, and you shouldn't be arguing!"

Wes gave her a sheepish grin. "We heard your alarm go off, sweetheart, so we knew you were awake. . . ."

"And we're not arguing," Emma muttered. "We're having a discussion."

"Uh-huh. Let me get this straight. Grandfather wants to take a shower, and you're trying to defrost a turkey in the tub. What happened to the fresh turkey, Emma?"

Emma sighed. "I got to the market just

before closing time yesterday, ready to pick up our fresh turkey, and was told by that addle-headed butcher he'd run out. Well, I won't go into what happened after that, but you'll find the results in the bathtub. I've seen many a Thanksgiving in my day, and a good many of them right here while I've been your granddaddy's housekeeper, but I've never had to defrost a turkey! I had to ask Mary Ellis at the checkout how to do it, and I've never been more humiliated in my life, especially when Penelope Davis was right behind me, with a twenty-pound *fresh* turkey in her cart. Come to find out, she got to the butcher shop ten minutes before me, and had snatched up the last one. Worse, she didn't even order it. She was going to roast a chicken, and changed her mind at the last minute. And if that isn't the ticket, she's only having three people for dinner. I told her we had a count of nine, including us, and tried to talk her into swapping, but she wouldn't hear of it. That's when I asked her why she needed a twenty-pound bird for three people, unless she was setting a place at the table for all her cats. If you can believe it, she actually got huffy!"

Wes tried to hold back the smile, and mischief danced in his blue eyes. "Good thing Jennifer was at the clinic when you brought the turkey home. And it's a good thing it was already plucked, or we'd be picking up feathers all over the house."

Emma snorted. "And a big help *he* was. He thought it was funny. He thought it was funny when I couldn't find room in the refrigerator too, because the frozen bird wouldn't bend. Well, you know what I mean. With a fresh turkey, you can sort of push it around and make room."

"How long will it take to defrost under running water?" Jennifer asked.

"Counting the time it's been in the refrigerator, about two more hours, and it has to be in the oven by eight. The way I see it, every minute counts. And that means no showers until after eight! I just know it's going to taste like one of those dried-out frozen dinners!"

"Nonsense," Wes said. "They flash-freeze turkeys these days to hold in the flavor, and with a good cook like you in the kitchen, nobody will know the difference."

Emma's frown faded into a weary smile. "Well, thank you for the compliment, but best you remember that when you have to carve old 'Tom' and can't cut through the skin." She shook her head. "The turkey is frozen, the storm is going to take off the roof, and I have a stomachache. I'm probably getting an ulcer!"

Wes winked at Jennifer. "Don't let her kid you. If she has an upset stomach, it's because she spent yesterday sampling all the side dishes she was cooking up. A Jell-O salad mold; sauce for the vegetables. Topping for the pies. The glaze for the yams. A spoon of this, a spoon of that, and by dinnertime, she was so full, she couldn't eat."

Emma wrinkled her nose, as though the mere thought of food turned her stomach.

"Have you taken the giblets out of the cavities?" Jennifer asked. "That might help speed things along."

"That's a nice way to say 'innards,' " Emma muttered. "And no, I haven't. Didn't even try. Just carrying it upstairs nearly froze my hands solid."

"Well, allow me," Wes said, heading for the bathroom. "I'm all for anything to hurry things up."

Emma gave a heartfelt sigh. "I wanted everything to be perfect today, Jennifer. I wanted it to be a Thanksgiving to remember."

"It doesn't have to be perfect, Emma, as long as we're together," Jennifer said gently. "But I still don't understand how you ended up with a frozen turkey when you ordered a fresh one."

"That's what I told Orris, among other things. I said, 'I've known you a good long time, Orris Ford. Probably going on close to five years now, ever since you moved down from Ainsworth and took old Greely's place behind that meat counter, and you know I always order a fresh turkey.' He told me he didn't know how it happened. He said he took inventory the day before, when the turkeys were delivered from North Platte, and that every fresh turkey that had been ordered was accounted for. And then he proceeded to tell me the young man who helps out in the butcher shop got into a car accident out on Route 5 the day before, and was in the hospital. He said he was so upset, he guessed things could have gotten mixed up, and that made me feel terrible. And then . . ."

"You two better come look at this!" Wes hollered from the bathroom.

Emma rolled her eyes. "Now what!"

Jennifer followed Emma into the bathroom, prepared to see her grandfather wrestling with the turkey. Instead, he was sitting on the edge of the tub, holding a diamond necklace in one hand and a soggy sheet of butcher paper in the other!

The two women's eyes opened wide. Jennifer sucked in her breath. "What on earth . . ."

"I was going to take out the giblets, and I found it stuffed in the breast cavity," Wes said, shaking his head in bewilderment.

Emma crossed her arms over her chest and scowled. "Mr. Wes, I don't have time for one of your practical jokes today. What is all this foolishness?"

Jennifer sensed that her grandfather wasn't joking. "Do you suppose those are *real* diamonds?" she asked.

"I don't know much about diamonds," Wes said, "but they sure look real to me. But how in the world did they get inside this turkey?"

It was a beautiful choker necklace, made up of several smaller diamonds with one large stone in the center. Jennifer didn't know that much about diamonds either, but she agreed with her grandfather. They looked very, very real.

"Well, that cuts it," Emma announced. "That old Tom is going out to the trash can where it belongs! Let the vultures pick it clean at the dump!"

Wes said, "That's not necessary, Emma. There is nothing wrong with the turkey."

Emma stood her ground. "I'd rather feed our guests macaroni and cheese than a turkey that's been handled by a thief!"

Aware that Emma was serious, and that Thanksgiving was going to end up a disaster if she didn't listen to reason, Jennifer said, "Grandfather is right, Emma. There is nothing wrong with the turkey."

Wes nodded. "And besides, we have no proof a thief put the necklace in the turkey."

Emma pushed a wisp of wiry brown hair off her forehead with the back of her hand, and snapped, "So I'm supposed to believe the butcher put the necklace in the turkey because he's handing out early Christmas gifts? Haven't you read *The Case of the Cooked Goose* by Noel Blackman? It's sitting right there on the bookshelf in the library, along with all those mystery novels Jennifer has been collecting over the years. A big-city bachelor attorney was found dead on his kitchen floor on Christmas Eve, holding a cooked goose. Come to find out, he'd picked up the wrong goose at the market, a goose that was stuffed with emeralds and intended for a fence, I might add. The scatterbrained attorney was in a hurry, and didn't think to look inside before he popped it in the oven. On Christmas Eve, while all the guests were in the living room waiting for dinner, the fence came in the back door, killed the attorney, and took the emeralds."

This time, Wes rolled his eyes. "You read too many mysteries, Emma."

"Might as well. Have to keep up with things. Our little town has had one blooming mystery after another for months. Why should all that change now? Maybe I should write my own series of mysteries, all about what goes on in Calico. Hrump! I'd probably get laughed right out of the publishers' offices, because they wouldn't believe any of it."

"Well, that's a fact," Wes said, looking at his watch. "No point calling the sheriff. He'll be here in a few hours . . ."

"Well, you'd better call him, because as long as that necklace is in this house . . ."

"I'll call him," Jennifer said. Emma might not be about to get a "perfect" Thanksgiving, but she was certainly going to get one to remember.

Wearing jeans and a dark blue sweatshirt, with her honey-colored hair tied up with a bit of yarn, Jennifer was chopping onions for the stuffing when the sheriff arrived at the back door.

"Come in!" Jennifer called. "It's open!"

Sheriff Jim Cody, a large, portly, grayhaired man who had been the sheriff for as long as Jennifer could remember, walked in, bringing a surge of wind and rain with him. He gave Jennifer a lopsided grin and said, "Hope all those tears are from the onions, and not because some other calamity has befallen you. You know, I was having the nicest dream when you called. All about Emma's good cooking, and a peaceful day in Calico. Should've known. My horoscope said it was going to be a lousy week." He took off his hat and raincoat, hung them on the coatrack near the door, and headed for the coffeepot. "Where is everybody?"

Jennifer looked at the sheriff through a shimmer of tears, and sniffed. "Emma is in the attic looking for extra vases for all the flowers she ordered, and Grandfather is in the bathroom with the turkey."

The sheriff's grin widened. "Should I ask?"

Jennifer smiled. "Guess I forgot to tell you the details. The turkey was frozen, and we're trying to defrost it in the bathtub under running water."

"Well, I guess that makes sense. Better than what Ida did the year we had a frozen bird. She just stuck it in the oven frozen, and we ate at midnight." He took a swallow of coffee and looked around. "So where is the necklace?"

"Over on the sideboard, along with the butcher paper it was wrapped in."

The sheriff walked over to the sideboard, picked up the necklace, and examined it carefully. "This is worth big bucks," he said with a grunt.

"Then you think the diamonds are real?"

"I'd bet my turkey dinner on it."

"You know, Sheriff, after I called you, I got to thinking. There has to be a reason why the necklace was in the turkey, and maybe Emma isn't so far off after all." Jennifer went on to tell him about *The Case of the Cooked Goose*, and waited for his reaction.

The sheriff frowned in thought, and then pursed his lips. "I guess it could've happened that way. But then the question would be, who's the thief? And who's the fence?"

"Maybe somebody put the necklace in the turkey before it was frozen and shipped to Calico," Jennifer said, dumping the chopped onions into a large bowl.

"Which would mean the thief, or his accomplice, works at the turkey packing plant in North Platte, and the fence, or the person who was supposed to receive the stolen necklace—assuming it was stolen—lives here in Calico. About all I can do at this point is call the authorities in North Platte. Maybe there was a jewel heist, or . . ."

His words trailed off as Emma walked into the kitchen carrying a large paper bag. "Good morning, Sheriff," she said, pulling vases out of the bag and lining them up on the table. "Sorry to bring you out in this weather, but that necklace doesn't belong here. It belongs in your office, locked up in your safe, until the owner is found. I have enough problems without worrying about the thief sneaking in and killing me where I stand."

The sheriff chuckled. "Jennifer told me about *The Case of the Cooked Goose.*"

Emma snorted. "Well, you know what they say. Truth is stranger than fiction, and living in Calico ought to prove that."

"If you'd like to take care of the flowers, Jennifer, I'll finish up the stuffing, *if* in fact, we end up with a turkey to stuff."

"We not only have a turkey to stuff, but I'd say it's a mighty fine-looking one," Wes said, carrying the turkey into the kitchen. He placed it on the counter and wiped his hands. "It's defrosted, clean as a whistle, and I blotted it with a towel. It's all yours, Emma." He smiled at the sheriff and shook his hand. " 'Morning, Jim. Sorry we had to call you out so early."

"And I'm sorry your morning was turned on end. This is one for the books, that's for sure, but Emma is right. The necklace belongs in my office safe until we can unravel the mystery. Meanwhile, it's Thanksgiving, and I told Ida I wouldn't be long. She's chin deep in pumpkin pies. Oh, and she wants to know who's coming for dinner besides us and Nettie. I told her I didn't think it was polite to ask, but you know Ida. She doesn't socialize much, and I'm sure she's worrying about what to wear. Should she dress for comfort, or to impress nobility?"

"Well, she doesn't have to worry," Emma said. "We haven't invited the president, or even the mayor. Just Ben Copeland and his wife, Irene, and Willy Ashton. That makes a total of nine smiling, friendly faces, and it doesn't much matter what anybody wears. Tell her I'm wearing one of my Sunday dresses, if that helps. Best you tell her I appreciate the fact she's making the pies too, Sheriff. It's one less thing we have to do."

"Yeah, well, after Ida carved up all those pumpkins on Halloween, she tossed the meat in the freezer, so I expect pumpkin pies, muffins, and cakes well into next year."

"You'll never get rid of your spare tire with all those calories," Jennifer teased.

"You'd better listen to her," Wes said, patting his firm stomach. "Without her expertise and all that prodding, and getting Emma to cook low-fat, low-calorie dishes, I'd still be 'the plump pastor' instead of 'the trim pastor' of Calico Christian Church."

"Uh-huh. I know, but I'm afraid calorie

counting will have to wait until after the holidays. Ida likes to bake, and I never could resist a Christmas cookie.

"I'll need a bag for the necklace, and I might as well take along the butcher paper. Don't think I'll be able to lift any prints, what with it washed clean and all, but you never know."

Five minutes later, the sheriff headed out the door carrying the bag, and Emma sighed with relief. "Now maybe we can get on with Thanksgiving, and put that unsettling incident behind us!"

Jennifer saw the look in her grandfather's eyes, and she knew exactly what he was thinking. Was this the end of the "diamond necklace incident"? Or was it only the beginning?

Chapter Two

Jennifer stood in front of the living room window and watched the shifting, puffy clouds play tag with the sun. Her favorite people would be arriving any moment to share in the Thanksgiving festivities, filling the day with happiness and love. She'd grown up with Willy Ashton, and although they had been separated off and on while she was away at veterinary school and he was in law school, they were still best friends. Maybe even more than friends. And dear Ben. He owned the Front Street veterinary clinic where she worked as his assistant, and she adored him. She adored his pretty, dark-haired wife, Irene too, and Nettie Balkin, who had been the sheriff's secretary, clerk, and dispatcher forever, and could put a smile on anybody's face with her friendly humor. And of course the sheriff was coming with his wife, Ida. Ida, a tall, thin woman who rarely smiled, was a little standoffish and critical of the town, and was forever after the sheriff to retire, but at least she'd agreed to come. All in all, the guest list was enough to brighten Jennifer's day, even if the sun hadn't finally decided to poke through the clouds.

Emma thought it was a miracle there had been a break in the storm at the very moment their guests were about to arrive. Jennifer thought it was a miracle they'd survived the morning.

Although everybody would be bringing a dish to add to the dinner table, Emma had still had to prepare the turkey and stuffing, candied yams, mashed potatoes and gravy, two vegetables, two salads, and all the little things, like homemade rolls and the pickles, olives, and celery on the relish tray that would be served before the feast. Jennifer and her grandfather tried their best to help, but had ended up underfoot more times than not, so they'd been delegated to other duties. They busied themselves with arranging the flowers, setting the dining room table with the china, silver, and crystal, and keeping logs on the fire.

And now, with everything ready, and the mouth-watering aroma of roast turkey wafting through the house, Jennifer knew it was going to be a wonderful day. Memories of holidays like this were to be cherished forever.

"You look beautiful, sweetheart," Wes said, joining Jennifer at the window. "The blue flowers in your dress are the same color as your eyes."

Jennifer kissed his cheek. "Thank you, Grandfather. I'm in jeans so much of the time at the clinic, it seems strange to be wearing a dress on a day other than Sunday."

"I know what you mean. Suits and Sundays go together too. I thought about wearing slacks, a sport shirt, and a sweater vest, but Emma wouldn't hear of it."

"That's because you look so handsome in your new blue suit."

"Uh-huh, and I'll be the only guy in a suit.

When Emma isn't looking, I'll take off my coat and tie."

"And you think you'll get away with that?"

Wes grinned. "I'll wait until Emma has her back turned."

"Well, you'll be the handsomest man here, with your coat on or off."

"That's what you say now, but you'll change your mind when that tall young fellow with the dark curly hair and blue eyes walks through the door." Wes sighed. "Listen to us, giving out compliments, when we should be praising Emma. Every year she amazes me, and all I can say is, she's done it again."

"And she enjoys every minute of it," Jennifer said warmly. "She's been singing for the last hour, so I think she's finally over her snit about the turkey. Or maybe she's realized by the wonderful aroma that it isn't going to taste like a dried-out frozen dinner after all."

Wes shook his head. "Boy, was that something. And I'll let you in on a little secret. As much as I've tried, I haven't been able to put the necklace out of my mind."

"Nor have I, but we'd better, at least for

now. Nettie is walking up the path, and her arms are loaded!"

Wes opened the front door. "You were only supposed to bring the cranberry sauce, Nettie," he scolded.

Nettie handed Wes two large bags and then shrugged. "Well, that's what you've got, cranberry sauce. Jennifer said something about having nine for dinner, so I thought I'd better double the recipe. Reminds me of the time I was learning to crochet, and tried to make a pair of booties for a friend's baby. I messed up somewhere, and the booties ended up big enough to fit the mother. Happy Thanksgiving, you two."

"Happy Thanksgiving," they both returned.

"You look terrific," Jennifer said, taking Nettie's wrap.

Nettie smoothed down her colorful print dress and grinned. "Now that's the way to start the party. Make me forget I'm twenty pounds overweight, and have gray hair and a double chin. Ah-ha, is that Emma I hear singing in the kitchen?"

"It sure is," Wes said.

"Do you suppose she'd mind if I put on an apron and gave her a helping hand?"

Wes chuckled. "Probably, but you can give it a try."

Within minutes, the rest of the guests had arrived, and the usual chaos prevailed. Everyone was talking at once, exchanging greetings and pleasantries. And Wes had been right. Although the women were wearing dresses, casual was the mode, with the men in slacks, sport shirts, and sweaters. Before Emma and Nettie could get the relish trays onto the side table in the living room, Wes had removed his coat and tie. Emma scowled at him, but didn't comment, because it wasn't important. After all, it was Thanksgiving. They were surrounded by good friends, and a special warmth, and that was all that mattered.

Jennifer had been dying to tell Willy about the necklace from the moment he walked in the door, but she had honored Emma's wishes. Emma was afraid if the guests found out about the necklace, nobody would eat the turkey.

Unfortunately, Emma hadn't sworn the sheriff to secrecy.

With everybody seated at the table, Wes had given the blessing and was carving the turkey. Sheriff Cody grinned at Willy and said, "So, Willy, what do you think about our puzzling diamond caper?"

Ida scowled. "You said you weren't going to discuss that today, Jim."

The sheriff tugged at the collar of his shirt like it was suddenly too tight. "Ah, yeah, well, it's kind of hard to ignore. And our young counselor here has a keen mind, just like Jennifer. I kinda figured they would've gotten their heads together by now, and had the whole mystery figured out."

Emma glared at the sheriff, and Jennifer cleared her throat. "Um, I think your wife is right, Sheriff Cody. Perhaps now isn't the time to discuss it."

"Whoa," Willy said. "I missed this. What diamonds?"

Wes began passing along plates heaped with turkey. "You lost the bet, Emma," he said with a chuckle. "I knew somebody was going to say something before the dinner was over."

Emma was clearly exasperated. "Well, if anybody is going to be doing the telling, it's going to be me. And I'll skip right over to the bottom line. We found a diamond necklace stuffed in the turkey."

Ben's rugged face broke into a smile. "I always knew Emma's cooking was worth a million bucks, but a diamond necklace?"

Irene poked him in the arm. "Ben!"

Nettie's eyes grew round. "Did you just say you found a diamond necklace in the turkey? Or am I hearing things?"

"You weren't hearing things," Wes said, and went on to explain.

Emma took the cranberry dish from the sheriff, handed over the mashed potatoes, and sighed. "It wasn't a pleasant experience. Getting stuck with a frozen turkey was bad enough."

Irene said, "No, I don't imagine that part of it was pleasant, even though the turkey turned out wonderful, Emma. But finding the necklace must have been exciting. I take it you think the diamonds are real?"

The sheriff nodded. "Real enough for me to wonder who put the necklace in the turkey, and why. Right now, it's in the safe in my office, and I'll begin a thorough investigation tomorrow."

Nettie grumbled, "Tomorrow, Jim? Are you aware tomorrow is the day after Thanksgiving, the start of the Christmas season, when everybody goes a little crazy shopping, Santa rides into town on a wagon, and the Christmas tree lot goes up in the Front Street Park?"

"Shouldn't matter," the sheriff said. "Right now all I can do is call the law in North Platte."

"Why North Platte?" Nettie asked.

"Because we think there is a chance the necklace was put in the turkey before it was shipped to Calico, and the packing plant is in North Platte. At least it's a place to start. Maybe there was a jewel robbery, or we'll luck out, and the necklace was reported stolen."

"Is it pretty?" Irene asked. "Well, I guess it must be, if it's made up of diamonds."

"It's beautiful," Jennifer said, giving Willy a curious glance. "You've been awfully quiet, Willy . . ."

Willy swallowed a forkful of candied yams and stabbed at his peas. "I was just thinking about Calico, and all that's happened over the last few months. Might as well have a diamond caper. Why not? Why stop the momentum?"

Jennifer squeezed his hand. "You're thinking about your mom, aren't you?"

Willy nodded. "She went to visit my aunt

in Florida, and she's coming home next weekend. She's very nervous about all the excitement in Calico. Wait until she hears about this!"

"Nothing to be frightened about that I can see," the sheriff said easily. "This time it doesn't concern the whole town, only the people directly involved—whoever they might be."

"*Everything* bizarre that happens here concerns the town," Ida mumbled. "And I know exactly how your mother feels, Willy. I can't imagine what happened to our quiet, peaceful town. Used to be nobody had to lock their doors, or . . ." She closed her mouth and shuddered.

"Have some stuffing," Emma said, handing Ida the bowl. "It's time we stop talking about unpleasantness, and get on with the festivities."

"I agree," Wes said, "or I'm going to have to say the blessing again, and start over. How's the job, Willy?"

"Same old same. Things get quiet around the holidays. About the most exciting thing that's happened lately was when two of the court clerks had sons on competing teams in pee-wee football. Judge Stoker got a kick out of all the boasting."

Ben spoke up. "Well, it isn't the same old same at the clinic. Late fall is a bad time for animals. Folks forget how cold it can get at night, and how susceptible their pets are to the elements. Jennifer and I had to work until after midnight last night trying to save a cat that had pneumonia."

"I didn't know cats could get pneumonia," Nettie said.

Jennifer replied, "It isn't common, but this was an older cat, suffering from asthma to begin with, and she'd been left out in the cold."

"So how do you treat something like that?" Willy asked.

"We used one drug to open up the bronchial tubes and another to combat the infection. We wanted to keep her a few days, but the owner wouldn't hear of it. So all we can do now is pray the cat makes it," Ben said.

"How is Tina Allen doing?" Nettie asked. "It can't be easy trying to keep up with her studies and working at the clinic."

Ben replied, "No, it isn't, but she's young and energetic."

"And determined," Jennifer added. "We

hired her as a general helper, and now she's like a third arm, even though her hours are limited. She's looking forward to next summer when she can work full time. In another two years, she'll be going off to college, and then vet school, and it's all she can talk about."

Wes smiled. "She reminds me of you, sweetheart. When you were that age, becoming a vet was all you could talk about too."

Emma said, "Speaking of animals, has anybody seen Elmer or Collin Dodd lately?"

Jennifer giggled. "How did you make that association, Emma?"

Emma shrugged. "Maybe it's the fact Elmer owns the dairy, and has all those Holstein cows. Or maybe it's the fact Collin Dodd is a vet. Or maybe it's because uncle and nephew are despicable men, and I think of them as predators."

The sheriff said, "You're not alone, Emma. The thought of Collin building an animal hospital out by the mall and trying to put Jennifer and Ben out of business weighs heavily on my mind."

"And the fact Elmer is going to run for mayor weighs heavily on mine," Nettie said.

Willy coughed lightly. "If I can have everybody's attention . . ."

"Uh-oh, sounds serious," Jim Cody said.

"Not serious, just important. I wasn't going to announce this until after Christmas, but I'd like to see a few smiling faces around the table, and hopefully this will do the trick. Elmer Dodd won't be running for mayor alone. I'm throwing my hat in the ring."

If Willy had announced he was giving up his law practice to take up anthropology in Egypt, he couldn't have gotten a more surprised reaction. Everybody seemed frozen for a few moments while his words sank in, and then came the laughter, hoots, and applause.

Wes stood up, lifted his glass, and said, "I propose a toast to Willy for his courage and spunk. That might mean the same thing to some people, but I see it a little differently. Courage is another word for determination, and spunk means he has the gumption to see it through."

"Hear, hear!" Ben said.

Willy blushed, but it was easy to see he was pleased. "I've been thinking about it for a long time, and finally decided Calico needs a responsible, honest man in the mayor's chair. We've put up with Mayor Attwater's apathy for years, but now the town is growing, and so are its problems. So why add to them by allowing Elmer Dodd that kind of power?"

"Amen," Emma said, giving Willy a brilliant smile. "You'll make a mighty handsome mayor, and a good one too."

"Does Elmer know?" Jim asked.

"No, and he won't until I make the formal announcement. Mayor Attwater is stepping down, and without an opponent, Dodd thinks he's a shoo-in."

"It could be a tough battle," Ben reasoned. "Elmer Dodd is a determined man."

"And unscrupulous," Nettie muttered. "I can see him using every underhanded tactic in the book to get into the mayor's office."

"And I'll be ready for him," Willy said.

The sheriff waved a fork. "You'll need a campaign manager."

Everybody looked at Jennifer, who was still in shock. When she could find her voice, she sputtered, "I-I'm happy for you, Willy, but personally I don't know the first thing about politics."

Wes grinned. "Don't underestimate yourself, Jennifer. I seem to recall a young lady who hadn't been home from vet school but a few weeks when she got involved with the planning of the town senior citizens' center. She was angry enough about the callous treatment of the senior citizens to take her complaint to the mayor, and was even talking about starting up a protest march. It doesn't take political knowledge to head up a campaign, sweetheart. It takes those qualities I mentioned before—determination and spunk."

"And it takes time," Willy added. "As much as I would like to have you as my campaign manager, Jenny, I couldn't ask you to give up your time at the clinic."

"She wouldn't have to," Ben said. "Like Tina Allen, Jennifer is young and energetic. She'll find the time."

Irene's eyes were narrowed in thought. "What about you, Willy? If you run for mayor, what will happen to your law practice?"

"In a town this size, I see no reason why I can't do both, as long as the cases I take don't cause a conflict of interest. And there isn't anything in the town charter that would prohibit me from running."

Emma said, "You have a lot of friends, Willy, but if you expect to compete with a wealthy man like Elmer Dodd you're going to need money for flyers and banners and pins and all those things that go along with a mayoral race. Well, you're looking at the lady who knows all about giving potlucks and bazaars and bake sales to raise money. Count me in."

"Me too," Ben said. "I've always wanted to wear one of those straw hats."

Within minutes, everybody had offered their services to Willy's campaign in one way or another. Even Ida, who liked to bake, said she would contribute to the bake sales.

"The election isn't until next November, so we have plenty of time," Willy said.

Emma clucked her tongue. "But it isn't too soon to start thinking about it, or planning. Can't you just see Elmer's face when he hears the news?"

For the next hour, the conversation centered around the campaign, until Emma brought out the pumpkin pies and fresh whipped cream and began serving up generous portions. That was when Nettie said, "You never did say how you ended up with that particular frozen turkey, Emma."

Emma replied, "To tell you the truth, I've been trying to forget about it, but I suppose it's like a cold. It's going to take its sweet time going away. I ordered a twenty-pound fresh turkey, and when I had to settle for frozen, there was only one left weighing twenty pounds. Sixteen pounds was the other choice, and I thought it would be too small. From the looks of the remains in the kitchen, I'd say I was right. Not that I mind, you understand. It does my heart good to know you all enjoyed the meal."

"What about you?" Irene asked. "You barely touched your food."

Emma shrugged. "I sampled a little bit of everything earlier on. Hmm, well now, just because we don't have a lot of leftovers doesn't mean there isn't enough turkey to make some nice sandwiches. I'll wrap up a little package for everybody to take home."

"You can skip me," Nettie said. "I'll have to fast for a week to make up for today." Her brows furrowed in thought. "Was your turkey wrapped like the other frozen birds?"

Emma's brows furrowed too. "No, now that you mention it. It was wrapped in butcher paper."

Nettie smiled smugly. "Just like the diamonds. Was there a weight written on the outside?"

"No. . . ."

"Uh-huh. Well, that suggests to me the turkey was fresh when it arrived from North Platte, and somebody at the market put the necklace in the turkey and tossed it in the freezer. Didn't you think it was odd that it wasn't wrapped like the other frozen turkeys?"

"No," Emma said, shaking her head. "I surely didn't, because I was upset. All I could think about was that blamed frozen chunk of poultry. I just knew I wouldn't be able to get it defrosted in time."

Irene asked, "Did Orris wait on you? Or was it that young assistant of his?"

"It was Orris, and that's something else. As angry as I was, I felt guilty too for giving him such a bad time. His helper had been in a car accident out on Route 5 the day before, and ended up in the hospital, so poor Orris had to handle everything himself. He had enough on his mind without all my bellyaching."

"Must have been that accident Tuesday afternoon," the sheriff said thoughtfully. "Deputy Pressman went on the call, and the state troopers took it from there. I knew there was an injury involved, but I had no idea it was Orris's assistant."

Nettie went on. "I can understand Orris being upset about the young man, and maybe even a bit flustered having to work alone at the meat counter during such a busy time, but wouldn't you think he would've noticed that the turkey wasn't wrapped like the others? And if the weight wasn't marked, how did he know it weighed twenty pounds?"

"By the feel of it, I would imagine," Emma said. "I saw no reason to question him."

Ida lifted her chin. "Well, while you people discuss the frozen turkey and the diamond necklace, my thoughts are with that poor young man in the hospital. Was he badly injured?"

Thoroughly chastised, Emma lamented, "Orris said something about a broken arm, broken nose, and some head injuries. Said he'd be in the hospital a few days."

"That sounds pretty serious to me," Ida said.

"Roger," Irene said. "The young man's name is Roger. I remember how happy Orris was the day he announced he'd hired an apprentice, to help ease the workload."

The sheriff wiped his mouth with a napkin. "Along with calling the authorities in North Platte, I think I'd better have a long talk with Orris. If Nettie is right, and the necklace was stuffed in the turkey after it arrived in Calico, the investigation will have to begin here, and I don't have to tell you what that could mean."

Ida scowled at her husband. "No, you certainly don't, Jim. It could mean hours and hours of overtime, while you wade through one lead after another. I was so hoping we could get through this holiday season without any more incidents. . . ."

It was raining again. Jennifer listened to it pounding down on the roof, and felt a sudden chill. If Nettie's theory were right, and if the necklace had been stolen, then the thief lived in Calico. Beyond that, she couldn't even begin to speculate.

It was after eight when Jennifer and Wes finished cleaning up the kitchen, and although they hadn't discussed it, they were both concerned. The last guest had barely gotten out the door, when Emma said she was going to bed. It wasn't like her. And it proved what Jennifer had suspected all day, that Emma wasn't feeling well.

At nine o'clock, Jennifer carried two cups of coffee into the study and sat down beside her grandfather on the brown leather couch. "I just checked on Emma, and she's asleep."

Wes put the book he was reading aside, and sighed. "She wore herself out, sweetheart. We should've insisted on doing more to help her."

"I don't think that's it, Grandfather. Emma thrives on hard work, especially around the holidays. I think she's ill. She barely touched her dinner, and I caught her holding her stomach a couple of times. If she isn't better in the morning, I think she should see a doctor, and I don't think it should be old Doc Chambers. I think she should go to the hospital."

Wes nodded. "You know, except for a cold or two, I can't remember a time when Emma was really ill. She's always been so healthy, and tough. . . ."

Jennifer gave Wes a hug. "I know, but she's also human, no matter what she would like us to believe."

Wes grew silent, and the concern in his

eyes was a reflection of her own. Emma Morrison was much more than a house-keeper. She was a member of the family, and they loved her.

Jennifer rested her head against her grandfather's shoulder, and closed her eyes. "Say a prayer, Grandfather?"

He took her hand and bowed his head. . . .

Chapter Three

It had been a slow morning at the clinic, and with no appointments scheduled for the rest of the day, Ben put the closed sign on the door after lunch. "Business is about what I expected, Jennifer. It's the day after Thanksgiving, and people are either home trying to recuperate after the big feast, or they are out taking advantage of all the sales. No appointments scheduled for to-morrow, either, so unless we have an emer-gency, I'll see you on Monday morning."

Jennifer took off her light blue lab coat, and sighed. "It really makes me wonder if

Calico can support two animal hospitals, Ben, especially during the winter months."

"I agree. Collin Dodd would be a lot smarter if he talked Elmer into getting rid of the resident vet at the dairy so he could take over there. That herd of Holsteins would keep him busy enough, and out of trouble."

"And off our backs too. But I can't see that happening. Collin visualizes building a state-of-the-art animal hospital and putting us out of business, and although I haven't wanted to think about it, he might succeed, Ben. He has a lot of money and the Dodd name to back him, and there are still a good number of Calico residents who frown on even the thought of using a female vet, or who simply refuse to take me seriously."

"Are you thinking about the Sorensons?" Ben asked.

"Well, aren't they a good example? They refused to let me look at their ailing cow, and although Mr. Sorenson went into great detail about how you've always been their vet, he couldn't fool me. He didn't want a woman administering to the cow. I'd like to be optimistic, but . . ."

"You're the one who said if Collin wanted

a fight, he'd get it," Ben said, shrugging into his rain slicker. "Come on, Jennifer. Yesterday your grandfather was talking about spunk and determination, so where are you hiding it now? Yesterday you were up, today you're down, and it's not like you."

Jennifer said, "Between Thanksgiving and Willy's exciting news, yesterday was special. But today . . . Maybe it's the gloomy weather. I wish it would snow."

"Well, you might get your wish. The weather forecaster said we could have snow by nightfall. Now, do you want to level with me? Doesn't your mood have something to do with the diamond necklace?"

"Maybe. I know it's silly, but . . ."

"Not so silly. Nor does it take much to see what's happening. The necklace was in your turkey; now it's in the sheriff's safe. Chances of finding the culprit, if it was stolen, are nil to none, and it's driving you crazy. You have a creative mind, young lady, and you're at your best when it's in overdrive. So let me make a suggestion. Stop by the sheriff's office when you leave here, and let him bring you up to date. You'll feel better. And I'll let you in on a little secret. It's been on my mind too, and last night after we got home, it was all Irene could talk about. She played supersleuth until midnight. I finally had to turn out the light, and pull the covers over my head. Then she kept saying, 'Ben, are you awake?' Let's face it, it's not every day of the week a diamond necklace gets stuffed into a Thanksgiving turkey, and it's not exactly easy to ignore."

"Well, it wasn't the topic of conversation at our house. Emma went to bed right after everybody left, and that wasn't like her, either. She's usually running on nervous energy after a dinner party, and chatters like a magpie. She'd complained of stomach pains earlier in the day, and she barely touched her dinner."

"Ah-ha, so that's why you've been calling home every half hour or so."

"Yes, it is, but I guess that was silly too. Emma was up before six this morning, full of energy, and said the discomfort in her stomach was gone. I had to believe her, because she ate a turkey sandwich for breakfast."

"Emma is a dear lady, and you care for her a great deal, Jennifer. We all do."

Jennifer gave Ben a hug. "I know, and I couldn't stand it if anything happened to her. Now, do you want to level with me? Do you want me to stop at the sheriff's office for my sake, or yours?"

Ben grinned. "Guess I'm pretty obvious, huh? Will you call me at home if you find out anything new and exciting?"

"I will. Have a good weekend, Ben."

"You too," Ben said, bracing himself for the onslaught of rain before he opened the door.

Sheriff Cody was on the phone when Jennifer walked into his office. Nettie was munching on a turkey sandwich, and by the look of pleasure on her face, she was no doubt enjoying every morsel.

Nettie looked up at Jennifer, and grinned sheepishly. "I know, I was the one who didn't want to take home any leftovers. Now I'm glad Emma talked me into it. Shows you even brilliant minds can make mistakes. You look chilled clean through, Jennifer. A cup of coffee might help warm you up."

"I can't stay, Nettie. I have some errands to run for Emma before I go home. Just stopped in to see how things are going. Any luck?"

"Jim has been talking to the boys in North

Platte off and on all morning. No record of a jewelry heist, and the necklace wasn't reported stolen."

"Is it possible it belongs to somebody in Calico?"

"Could be," the sheriff said, hanging up the phone. "That's why I decided to call John, Jr." When Jennifer opened her mouth to protest, he held up a hand. "Hear me out, Jennifer. Without a report that the necklace was stolen or missing, and with nothing on the state computer to suggest a jewelry heist, I ran out of options."

"So you gave the information to John, Jr., to print in the *Calico Review*, hoping the owner will read about it and come forward, right?"

"That's right. It might not solve the mystery of how the necklace got into the turkey, but I'll be satisfied if I can return it to the rightful owner. I didn't give the description to John, Jr., but the owner will know what it looks like, and that will be good enough for me."

Nettie muttered, "The person who put the necklace in the turkey, or the person who was supposed to receive it, will be able to describe it too, Sheriff."

"I don't think they'd have the guts to come forward, Nettie."

"Maybe not, but I still think you'd better be prepared for a long line of takers."

Jennifer asked, "What if the opposite happens, Sheriff, and nobody claims the necklace?"

"Then I'll keep it in the safe, list it along with all the unclaimed paraphernalia in the property room, and put it on the auction block come spring."

Jennifer thought about John Wexler, Jr., who had taken over his father's newspaper after coming home from college, and who had the tenacity, and arrogance, of ten men. "John, Jr., will run with it, Sheriff. You know he'll blow it all out of proportion."

"Maybe, but I have to take that chance. I didn't give him the whole story. I just told him a Calico resident found a diamond necklace stuffed in a turkey, and we'd like to know who it belongs to."

"Did you talk to Orris Ford?"

"I did. I didn't give him the details, either. I just said a resident found a diamond necklace in one of the frozen turkeys he sold on Wednesday, and if he could shed some light on the matter, I'd be most appreciative. He was surprised to say the least, and defensive. Like he thought I was accusing him. I didn't say anything about the possibility of the necklace getting stuffed in a fresh bird at this end, but I did ask him if he remembered anybody hanging around the meat counter after the turkeys were delivered. Orris said it wouldn't have mattered who was hanging around the meat counter, or why, because he put all the fresh turkeys in the refrigerator in the back room."

"What about Roger?" Jennifer asked. "Was he there when the turkeys were delivered?"

"He was."

"What time was that?"

"Around two."

"Have you talked to him?"

The sheriff nodded. "I stopped by the hospital after I talked to Orris, but kept the questions brief. He's only been in town a few months. He looks like he's been run over by a tractor, and is feeling pretty miserable. He was driving Orris's truck, and that makes it worse. He feels guilty because he was speeding."

"How did it happen?"

"Orris sent Roger out to the Butler farm

to deliver a fresh turkey. . . ." He looked at his notes. "That was about three. It happened when he was on his way back to town. A car traveling east on Route 5 tried to pass, and clipped a back bumper. Roger lost control, and rammed a tree. He was lucky. It could've been a lot worse."

"And the other car?"

"The driver ran off the road and sideswiped a fence. No injuries other than a few bumps and bruises."

Jennifer lined up all the facts in her mind and considered the possibilities for a moment before she said, "Does the back room behind the butcher shop have an outside door?"

"I know what you're thinking, and it occurred to me too. It does, but Orris said it was locked. Always keeps it locked except for deliveries."

"Then you only have two suspects, Sheriff. Orris and Roger."

"Orris has been a solid member of our community for at least five years, Jennifer. And he has the kind of face that's easy to read. I scratched him off the list first thing."

"Okay, but what about the apprentice? Roger . . ."

"Roger Nessler."

"Roger Nessler," Jennifer repeated. "He's only been in town a few months, and who else had the opportunity? He could have stuffed the necklace in one of the turkeys while Orris was out front waiting on a customer, and he had one hour between the time the turkeys were delivered and when he left for the Butlers'."

"Have you figured out why?"

Jennifer grinned. "That's your job."

Nettie bobbed her head. "Roger Nessler doing it makes more sense to me than somebody lurking around the meat counter, trying to get into the back room."

When the phone rang, Jim picked it up with a sigh. "Sheriff Cody . . . Uh-huh. The basement is flooded? I'm sorry to hear that, but I'm afraid I can't help you out. Not the storm? Well, you'd better call the water company. Maybe you have a broken pipe . . . Uh-huh. Well, you have a good day too." The sheriff hung up and ran a hand over his eyes. "That's the way it's been all day, Jennifer. Along with all the calls to and from North Platte, the phone has been ringing off the hook. The streets are slick, so we've had a dozen fender benders. One lady misplaced her Christmas packages at the Mercantile, thought somebody had swiped them, and caused a scene. And the crazy Wilson brothers got into a hassle in the candy shop over a pound of saltwater taffy. And that's just for starters. My deputies have been going around in circles, trying to keep up with it all.

"Okay, so where were we? Uh-huh, Roger. So you both think he's our boy. Can't say the thought didn't occur to me too. I asked Orris about him, but he couldn't tell me much. Said he's a hard worker, comes from Lincoln, likes to bowl, and he lives in the Cottonwood Apartments near the bowling alley. I plan to do some digging—" The phone rang again, and the sheriff wearily shook his head. "Sheriff Cody . . ."

"I'd better be going," Jennifer said to Nettie. "If anything earth-shattering happens, let me know."

Nettie grinned. "That's a ten-four, young lady. And you take care out there, you hear?"

Jennifer nodded and headed for the door, bracing herself for the surge of cold. It had stopped raining, and the temperature had dropped. Now the gray, swirling clouds held the promise of snow.

But the weather hadn't stopped the shoppers, or the Santa who was standing in front of the Mercantile ringing a little brass bell. This year, the focus was on the Toys for Tots drive and Meals on Wheels for housebound senior citizens.

Jennifer dropped a five-dollar bill into the bucket beside Santa, wished him a Merry Christmas, and walked into the Mercantile, carrying Emma's long list. The official Christmas season had started at home too, and just the thought of it was enough to finally put a smile on her face.

"Red, green, and white tissue paper," Jennifer said, removing the items from the first bag. "Oh, and they had a sale on tinsel and red velvet bows."

Emma was perched on a step stool, poking around in the cupboard above the refrigerator. "You didn't forget the Scotch tape, did you?"

"No, I didn't. What on earth are you doing up there, Emma?"

"Trying to find the tureen."

"I knew we were having turkey soup the minute I opened the front door. It smells wonderful. I take it you're feeling better?"

"I felt better this morning, Jennifer. Just like I told you every time you called. But I appreciate your concern. Hmm. Where is that tureen? I don't think I loaned it to anybody . . ."

"Let me look for it, Emma. It's probably tucked in the back, and you're a little short on one end."

Emma gratefully got down off the step stool, and fanned her face with her apron. "It's either too hot or too cold. This morning, I was freezing to death, and now it's so toasty I can scarcely breathe. Your granddaddy says it's my imagination. I say it's the thermostat on that blasted heater."

Jennifer climbed to the top rung of the ladder, and began sorting through things in the cupboard. "Where is Grandfather, Emma?"

"At the church, doing some paperwork. He says it's going to snow."

"It's about time. Oh, I know we had that snowstorm in October, but I wasn't ready for it then."

"And now you are? Well, I'll remind you of that the first time you have to shovel the walkway to get to your Jeep. My, my, isn't this pretty."

Emma was holding a crystal snowflake ornament she'd taken out of the bag from the Mercantile. Jennifer grinned. "Couldn't resist it, Emma."

"And what's this?"

"Looks like a gavel to me," Wes said, strolling into the kitchen.

Jennifer smiled down at her handsome grandfather. "That's exactly what it is. I'm going to give it to Willy for Christmas. Just my way of wishing him good luck in the mayoral race." She pulled out the soup tureen and handed it down to Emma. "You're hair is wet, Grandfather. Is it raining again?"

Wes patted his white hair. "Nope. It's snowing."

Jennifer climbed down and gave him a hug. "Then everything is perfect. The clinic is closed until Monday, so all I have to do is enjoy the snow, your company, and the long weekend."

Wes winked at Emma. "You notice she

hasn't mentioned the diamond necklace? Do you suppose that means the sheriff has solved the mystery, and that the necklace has been returned to the owner?"

"I think it means the necklace is still sitting in the sheriff's safe, and the mystery is still a mystery," Emma retorted.

"Is that true?" Wes asked Jennifer.

"Yes, unfortunately. The necklace hasn't been reported stolen or missing in North Platte, and there is no record of a jewelry theft. So the sheriff is going on the assumption the owner lives in Calico. He called John, Jr.—"

"Uh-oh," Emma said. "That might be opening one big can of worms."

"I know, but it was a chance he had to take. He didn't give John, Jr., any of the details. He just said somebody found a diamond necklace stuffed in a turkey. He's hoping the owner will read the story and come forward."

Emma snorted. "I can see a line reaching all the way to the river. Suddenly, everybody will want to claim the necklace."

"It's possible that could happen, but the sheriff didn't give John, Jr., a description, so only the owner will be able to identify it."

"What happens if nobody can identify it?" Wes asked.

"Then it will be included in the next county auction."

Emma put the tureen in the sink, filled it with soapy water, and sighed. "Even if the owner comes forward, we'll probably never know how the necklace got in the turkey, or why. I was too busy to really think about it yesterday, and I was feeling a mite under the weather last night, but this is a new day, and I'll admit it's been on my mind."

Wes chuckled. "Come clean, Emma. Why don't you admit you're creating a plot for one of those mystery books you're planning to write."

Emma scowled. "Laugh if you want, but *somebody* put that necklace in the turkey, and there had to be a good reason. Did the sheriff talk to Orris?"

"Yes . . ."

"And?" Emma prodded.

"It's only speculation, mostly on my part."

"That's good enough for me, sweetheart. Let's hear it."

Jennifer gave them a condensed version

of her conversation with the sheriff, and concluded with, "So Roger Nessler seems to be the prime suspect. He had an hour between the time the turkeys were delivered, and Orris sent him out to the Butler farm. One hour full of chaos, while the turkeys had to be logged in and stored in the refrigerator, and customers clamored at the counter for service."

"It makes sense to me," Emma said.

"That's what Nettie said. A lot more sense than somebody lurking around, waiting to stuff the necklace in a turkey. But even if we have the 'who,' we don't know why."

Emma announced, *"The Case of the Cooked Goose.* Either Roger stole the necklace or got it from somebody else, and the fence was supposed to get that turkey."

"Or it wasn't a fence," Jennifer reasoned. "It's possible the necklace was simply supposed to go to one of Calico's citizens."

"Who would have to be as crooked as Roger Nessler."

Wes said, "If you're right about this, we have one consolation. The number-one suspect is stuck in the hospital, so he can't skip town."

"And it could also mean there is one angry somebody here in Calico," Emma returned.

"Maybe that angry somebody or other will visit Roger in the hospital, or call him—" The doorbell rang, and Jennifer's words were cut off.

Emma frowned. "Are we expecting company?"

"I'll get it," Wes said. "Maybe Willy changed his mind about sharing our leftovers."

But it wasn't Willy. It was Sheriff Cody, and from the look on his face, Jennifer knew the news wasn't good. As the snow melted on his hat and jacket, he shuffled from one foot to the other. Emma was watching him intently. "Well?" she asked finally. "Somehow, I don't think this is a social call, Sheriff."

The sheriff sighed. "It isn't. I just came from the hospital. Roger Nessler has disappeared."

Silence followed his announcement. Finally Emma said, "Disappeared? But he was injured. He was in the hospital."

"That's right, and he was in no condition to get up and walk out, but he did. A nurse went in to give him pain medication around two, and he was gone. All I can say is, everything is staying about par with the investigation. Nobody saw anything or heard anything. I checked with Orris, and he hasn't seen him, and he isn't at his apartment."

Jennifer said, "He was using Orris's truck to deliver the turkey to the Butler farm, so what about his car?"

"It's still parked behind the market. The whole thing presents some kind of picture, when you think about it. His clothes got chewed up in the accident, which meant he left the hospital in one of those abbreviated gowns. His head was wrapped, face all black and blue, and his arm was in a sling. And nobody saw him. Makes you wonder."

"Sounds like he had help getting out," Wes said.

Jennifer said, "It also sounds like he left in a hurry."

The sheriff nodded. "So the big question is, why?"

Emma was bobbing her head. "Just like I said. The person who was supposed to receive the necklace is hopping mad, and Roger ran for cover."

"Or all my questions scared him off."

Trying to understand what it meant, Jennifer asked, "Was he in a private room?"

"He was."

"First the diamond necklace, and now a missing suspect!" Emma exclaimed.

"I know this is probably a silly question, but how are you going to handle it, Jim?" Wes asked.

"I'll have to start over from the beginning. Might end up treating it as an abduction, because that's a definite possibility."

Emma shuddered. "Well, you can't start over from the beginning until morning, so why don't you just put everything on hold for now, and sit a spell. Have a bowl of turkey soup. You look like you could use something hot and nourishing."

"That would be nice, Emma, if it isn't any trouble. The wife is feeling a little under the weather, and I'd end up nuking a dinner in the microwave."

Jennifer walked to the window. The snow was falling heavily now, with a few errant flakes clinging to the pane. The sheriff might be able to put the investigation on hold for a few hours, but it wouldn't stop him, or any of them, from thinking. A stolen diamond necklace was one thing. A missing suspect was quite another.

Chapter Four

Bundled up in a parka, jeans, and boots, Jennifer stood at the edge of the road and watched Ben trudge up the snowy embankment. All around them, blinking red, blue, and yellow lights cast an eerie glow as rescue workers attempted to extract the occupants from the overturned van. She'd received the emergency call from Ben just before the alarm had gone off, and had shrugged into her clothing while she listened to his chilling words. A van pulling a horse trailer had gone off the road near "Deadman's Curve" on Route 5, and the state troopers were in a quandary over what to do with the injured horse. Five minutes after the call Jennifer was on her way, thankful for her four-wheel-drive vehicle, because it was still snowing and visibility was nearly zero.

Jennifer couldn't see the horse trailer from where she was standing, but she could see the grim expression on Ben's face.

Ben greeted her and stomped the snow off his boots. "It's one ugly scene," he muttered.

"Are they alive?"

"They are, but the woman is unconscious. The man thinks his ankle is broken. They missed the curve, and went right over. The big problem now is trying to get them out. They might have to use the 'Jaws of Life.'"

"And the horse?"

"Mr. Pippin. That's another story, and we've got a problem. When the state troopers realized the horse was wearing a halter and headstall, they thought they would do us a favor, and get it out of the trailer. Well, it reared up and bolted. That was the last they saw of it."

"Then the horse wasn't injured."

"They assumed it was injured because of the ruckus it was making and the serious-ness of the accident, but now they aren't sure, though one trooper thought he saw it limping."

"Even if it isn't injured, we're dealing with fear and shock. It won't survive long in this weather, Ben. . . ."

"I know. The tow truck driver used a winch to pull the trailer up to the road. It's dented up, and the wheels are out of line a bit, but we'll be able to use it to transport the horse, if we're lucky enough to find it."

"Transport it where? We don't have the facilities for a large animal at the clinic."

Ben heaved a ragged sigh. "Guess we could take it to the stable. You know Max Calder—if he doesn't have an available stall, he'll build us one."

Jennifer thought about her beautiful chestnut mare Tassie, snug and secure in her stall at the stable, and her heart twisted. She couldn't bear the thought of any animal frightened, lost, and alone in a storm. "Was the horse wearing a blanket?"

"No, but I found one in the trailer. It probably got tossed in the accident."

Jennifer looked out at the sea of white around them, and at the dramatic scene being played out at the bottom of the gully.

She shivered. "Did the troopers say which way the horse was headed?"

"South. Nothing but open fields in that direction until Walston Road, then a smattering of farms. I figure if the horse keeps on a straight course, we should catch up with it eventually. It's getting light, and the snow has let up a little, so that should help. I haven't got a hitch on my truck, so we'll have to hook the trailer up to your Jeep."

"What about your truck?"

"I'll have one of the deputies drive it back to town. We'd better get going, Jennifer. There isn't anything we can do here."

Fifteen minutes later, with her hands clamped to the wheel and every nerve in her body tense, Jennifer nearly lost control of the Jeep trying to make the turn onto Walston Road, because the trailer kept veering to the right. When she had corrected the problem enough to continue on, she muttered, "This is crazy, Ben. Even if we find the horse, it would be suicide to try to transport it all the way to town in that cockamamie trailer."

"Then I guess we'd better find us a friendly farmer."

Jennifer had the heater turned on high,

but her teeth were still chattering. "It's getting colder."

"I know," Ben said, wrapping his parka closer around him. "The temperature must be in the teens. Maybe lower." He took off his gloves and blew on his fingers. "You know, we didn't get much sleep after you called last night. It's hard to believe Roger Nessler walked right out of the hospital in broad daylight. We stayed up talking until well after midnight, again. Irene thinks he was abducted, and the culprit is going to kill him to keep him quiet. I think she watches too much TV. I'm more inclined to believe the sheriff scared him off, and he ran."

"If he did, he had to have had help. The sheriff hopes a background check on Roger might turn up some answers, and—Oh, Ben, look!" Jennifer had rounded a curve, and the horse was standing in the road directly in front of them.

Jennifer brought the Jeep to a crawl, and then stopped. "I don't want to spook him."

"I don't think we have to worry about that. Looks like a frozen statue, and you see the way he's holding his head? He's about ready to go over."

Jennifer and Ben quickly approached the

dazed horse, talking to it softly. It nickered in return, blowing out puffs of hot vapor.

"We're here to help you, boy," Jennifer said soothingly, stroking the horse's quivering flesh. "Easy, now. That's the way."

"Good, Jennifer," Ben said. "Keep him calm and occupied while I take a quick look at him. I want to get him to shelter, but I want to make sure he's not injured."

Jennifer continued to soothe the horse while keeping a sharp eye on Ben's movements. "I notice the weight is evenly distributed on all four legs, Ben, so I don't think it's a leg injury. But he's definitely a frightened and very cold horse."

"He's got some small cuts and bruises on his right flank. I can't tell if they're from the accident or from running through brush. I want to clean those wounds as soon as possible and get some antibiotic ointment on."

Within minutes, they had the horse covered with the blanket. He offered no resistance as Ben opened the tailgate and Jennifer secured him in the trailer.

"Now what?" Ben asked, climbing into the Jeep beside Jennifer.

"Cracker Martin's farm isn't too far away.

He gets up early, and I know he'd be more than willing to help."

"Sounds good to me." Ben smiled. "Irene mentioned Cracker just the other day. Said he stopped by the senior citizens' center with a load of wood, and offered his services in the kitchen for Thanksgiving dinner. Same with Christmas. You know, you're the one responsible for turning that old recluse into a solid member of our community. And from what I've heard, he's even fixing up the old homestead."

"He was ready, Ben. All I did was push a little. I've been seriously thinking about getting him another dog. I know it would never take his old dog's place, but he needs more than his new friends at the senior citizens' center. He needs a full-time companion, something to love. He loved his wife very much, and he loved that dog, but now it's time to move on. And I think he knows it."

Ben sighed. "It's sad. But Cracker is lucky he has a friend like you who cares about him."

Jennifer felt her throat tighten as she thought about the sweet old man. "Well, maybe he also needs another 'man's best friend.'" She slowed the jeep. They had reached the road to Cracker Martin's farm, and only had a mile or so to go.

"Well, if this ain't a treat!" Cracker said, pouring coffee into three earthenware mugs. "I was gonna skip making a pot of coffee this morning, but something told me to make it. Cream and sugar is right there on the table. Help yourselves."

They were sitting in Cracker's toasty kitchen, and Jennifer looked around appreciatively. The walls were freshly painted in pale yellow, and he had a new flowered tablecloth on the old oak table. "The house looks wonderful, Cracker, and so do you."

Cracker flushed. "I keep busy, and that keeps me from thinking about my creaking bones. Keeps me from getting too lonely."

"We all know how you feel, Cracker. . . . Thanks again for the use of your barn. The horse will be fine now, though I don't know how long you'll have to keep him. I'll talk to Max at the stable. If he has a vacant stall, and will let us use one of his trailers to transport him . . ."

"Don't matter none," Cracker said, trying to smooth down his gray hair that was going every which way. "I got plenty of hay, and as long as he don't mind the chickens pecking around, or the pigs getting vocal, or Daisy Cow blowing in his ear, he'll do okay." He shook his head. "That's mighty nasty business. Folks drive along that stretch of road fast as the dickens, and in all kinds of weather. If those two in the van are still alive, they're lucky. Locals?"

"No," Ben said. "They were on their way from Grand Island to Scottsbluff. And I agree with you about that stretch of road."

"Nasty business. 'Bout as nasty as the weather. 'Course, the weather don't bother me none. If my truck gets stuck in a snowbank, I've got that old snowplow out behind the barn, and if I have to end up driving it, I will. I'll get to where I'm going, and be helping the road crews at the same time."

"That's one way to look at it," Ben said. "I heard you spent Thanksgiving at the senior citizens' center, Cracker, and were a big help in the kitchen."

Cracker snapped his suspenders and grinned. "Guess that pretty little wife of yours has been keeping you up to date. She's a wonder, organizing this and organizing that. We had a good time, and Christmas should be a hoot. Amy Loring plays the piano, and we're gonna exchange gifts, and have a sing-along."

"Will you be coming to the annual Christmas party?" Jennifer asked.

"Wouldn't miss it . . . Well, guess that was a dumb thing to say. I haven't been to those Christmas doings in a long time. Not since my Addy died."

Jennifer reached across the table and squeezed his callused hand. "You don't have to explain, Cracker."

"Guess I don't, 'cause you always seem to understand. Is your grandpa gonna be Santa again this year?"

"Yes, he is, and he's looking forward to it."

"My Addy used to say your grandpa was an angel 'cause he could preach a sermon at ten, put on the Nativity in the church social hall at two, and be Santa for the kids at the Grange at five. I remember one year when my old dog was a pup. Addy wanted to go to the Christmas party, but didn't want to leave the puppy at home, 'cause he was in his chewing stage. Figured if she worked it right, he could be a part of things."

Jennifer smiled. "I remember it too. Addy tied a Santa hat on the puppy's head, and taught him to carry a basket of candy canes in his mouth. I'll never forget what a hit he made with the kids."

"I still got that Santa hat, put away with Addy's things. . . ."

Jennifer swallowed around the lump in her throat. "Have you thought about getting another dog, Cracker?"

"Yeah, I have. Out of respect for my old dog, though, I wouldn't want another one like him. I'd want something different; maybe a female dog, or a smaller one." He smiled wistfully. "Got some sweet rolls to go with that coffee."

"Sounds good," Ben said.

"I'll pass," Jennifer said, looking at her watch. "I should call home . . ."

Cracker waved a hand. "There's the phone. You're the one who had it put in. I never use it. Waste of money."

Jennifer walked over to the phone and punched in her number. "You live alone, and you're quite a distance from town, Cracker, so having a phone is important." She frowned. "That's strange. Nobody is answering."

Cracker said, "Maybe they went out Christmas shopping." He squinted up at the clock on the wall. "Nope, guess that's not it. The stores ain't open yet."

"Were they up when you left?" Ben asked.

"No, they weren't. I didn't have time to leave a note, but this isn't the first time I've been called away on an emergency. I'm sure Grandfather heard the phone." She hung up and bit her lip. "Something must have happened. . . ."

"Are you wondering if Emma has taken a turn for the worse?"

"I can't help it, Ben. She was okay yesterday, or at least she said she was. She hasn't been feeling well, Cracker, and she's so stubborn."

"Want me to call the hospital?" Ben asked.

Jennifer shook her head, and dialed the operator. A few minutes later, she was talking to the hospital switchboard, and listening to the words she prayed she wouldn't hear. Emma had been admitted to the hospital with severe stomach pains.

When she could gather her thoughts, she said, "M-my grandfather—Wes Gray. He must be in the hospital. If you can page him . . ."

The operator transferred Jennifer to another extension, and then Wes was on the line. The concern in his voice, and his words, tore at her heart.

"I heard the phone early this morning, sweetheart, and knew you had an emergency by the way you rushed out. The alarm was about to go off anyway, so I got up. I . . . Well, I went down to the kitchen, set to make a pot of coffee, and heard Emma moaning in her room. I found her doubled over on the floor. I called for the ambulance, but it was out on Route 5, picking up a couple of accident victims. So, I did the only thing I could. I loaded Emma in my car and brought her here straightaway. It's her gallbladder, and they're getting her ready for surgery.

"I talked to the doctor, sweetheart, and he said she's a healthy lady, and he sees no reason for concern. It's a relatively simple operation, and she shouldn't have to stay in the hospital more than a week."

Simple? There was nothing simple about surgery, Jennifer thought. Any surgery! In one sentence, she told Wes where she was and why, and that she would get to the hospital as soon as she could.

By the time she hung up, Ben was already in his parka, waiting by the door.

"It's her gallbladder," Jennifer said, shrugging into her wrap. "I hate to rush off like this, Cracker, but . . ."

"You never mind about that. And don't you fret about the horse, either. He'll be fine, and so will Emma. You'll see."

Jennifer gave Cracker a hug, and then hurried to catch up with Ben.

"I'll drive," Ben said, after he unhitched the trailer. "You just hang on and pray, because this is gonna be one unpleasant ride."

Jennifer prayed all the way to town while Ben maneuvered the Jeep Cherokee over the treacherous roads. But it wasn't until she was in Wes's arms in the hospital waiting room that tears finally streamed down her cheeks. "We should have taken her to the hospital Thursday night, Grandfather."

"She would've put up a fuss, Jennifer, and that would've made things worse. Well, she's in good hands now, and all we can do is wait."

"Did the doctor say how long it will be?"

"No, but it shouldn't be too much longer now. She's been in surgery over an hour."

Jennifer walked to the window. She could

see the town, blanketed with snow, and the bridge that spanned White River, murky now, under a dark gray sky. If only the sun would shine . . .

"She's tough," Wes said, putting an arm around her shoulder.

"I know, but so many things can go wrong. I keep wondering if I missed something. Maybe she's been in pain all along, and I was too busy to notice."

"Shh," Wes soothed. "Even if she was ailing, she wouldn't have let us know."

Ben was telling Wes about the accident on Route 5 when the doctor walked in. He was a portly man with a wide smile, and after shaking hands with the threesome, he announced that the surgery had been successful. "She'll be in recovery for an hour or so, so you might as well relax. The cafeteria serves a pretty good breakfast, and the coffee is strong."

Wanting to hug the doctor, Jennifer asked, "How long will she be in the hospital?"

"Four to five days. The prognosis is excellent."

Ben said, "There was an accident earlier

out on Route 5. A young couple drove their van into a gully. Any word on them?"

Jennifer added, "They were pulling a horse trailer. Ben and I are vets, and we took care of the horse."

"Ah-ha, well, that solves that little problem. Mr. and Mrs. Masterson have been quite concerned about the horse. They were brought in about an hour ago. Mrs. Masterson has a concussion and has been admitted as a precaution, but Mr. Masterson escaped with only a sprained ankle and minor abrasions. They were very, very lucky. Perhaps if you talk to them, it will put their minds at ease. Apparently the horse was a gift from Mr. Masterson's mother."

Ben squeezed Jennifer's shoulder. "I'll take care of it, Jennifer. Why don't you go on down to the cafeteria with Wes, and try to relax."

Jennifer and Wes headed for the cafeteria, but she knew they wouldn't be able to relax until they could see Emma. They'd reached the elevator when Wes said, "How about taking a little detour? The chapel is on the second floor."

For the first time, Jennifer noticed her grandfather's disheveled appearance and the lines of fatigue around his eyes. Her love for him spilled forth. "I'd like that," she said softly, and took his arm.

"You can't tell me it wasn't that blasted turkey!" Emma exclaimed through dry, cracked lips. "I knew I should've tossed it out!"

Emma was trying to drink water through a squiggly straw, and fighting Jennifer because she wanted to hold the glass.

"It wasn't the turkey," Wes said, giving Emma a winsome grin. "Because nobody else took sick."

Emma snorted. "Well, you'd better not tell me it's old age."

"It's not that either," Jennifer said. "The doctor said you've had the condition for some time. It's called chronic cholecystitis, frequently brought on by the ingestion of fatty foods. And it's almost always associated with gallstones. You had quite a number of them, Emma. So I have a hard time believing you didn't have some sort of discomfort before."

"Well, maybe I did, but it wasn't bad. Not enough to cause a fuss."

"Well, your illness has caused quite a

fuss," Jennifer said. "We've called just about everybody, so I would imagine you'll be getting a lot of flowers and cards."

"Won't mind that none. Hmm. Do you suppose I'm near the room where—" She lowered her voice. "Do you suppose I'm near the room where Roger Nessler was a patient?"

Jennifer exchanged glances with Wes, and shook her head. "Roger Nessler's disappearance is the *last* thing you should be thinking about, Emma."

"Well, am I?"

"This is the surgical floor," Wes said. "Roger Nessler didn't have surgery."

"Just broken bones," Emma muttered. "What day is this?"

Wes chuckled. "It's still Saturday, Emma. You've only lost a few hours."

Her eyes narrowed. "What have they got in that thing going into my arm? It better not be pain medication. I don't want none of that. Want to be wide awake . . ."

Emma's eyes were drooping, and minutes later, she was snoring.

"She's going to be impossible," Jennifer said, bending over to kiss her cheek.

Wes brushed a strand of hair away from

Emma's forehead. "I know, and I wouldn't want her any other way. Let's go home, sweetheart, and tackle that list of chores Emma has up on the bulletin board."

Emma stirred, and murmured, "Don't forget the box of decorations on the hall shelf. It's taped and marked CRÈCHE and MISCELLANEOUS. And don't forget to throw out that blasted turkey carcass. . . ."

It was late Saturday afternoon before Jennifer and Wes finally had the chance to sit down at the kitchen table and take a well-deserved break. It had been difficult walking into the house and not hearing Emma's nonstop chatter, but the sun had finally poked through the clouds, lifting their spirits. Keeping busy had helped too, and so far, they'd managed to decorate the living room, dining room, and kitchen.

Wes took a sip of coffee, and sighed. "Emma didn't say, but I wonder if she finished her Christmas shopping."

"She did. She has everything wrapped too, and stuffed in her closet. But I know she hasn't gotten to the Christmas cards. Maybe she would like to have them at the hospital. It would give her something to do."

Wes added *cards* and *address book* to the list he'd started hours before. "Cards. Okay, and I'd better put down *box in the hall*, because the crèche isn't in it."

"Did you check the attic?"

"Not up there. Can't find the Christmas tree stand, either, and the Christmas cookie cutters."

"Are you thinking about baking cookies, Grandfather?"

"Maybe in a week or two. I can see the twinkle in your eyes. Don't think I can, huh? Well, I'll have you know when your grandmother Geneva was alive, I used to do all the cookie making. Seems like yesterday, and I can tell you right now, I haven't forgotten how, though I don't suppose it'll be an easy task what with Emma giving out orders."

"And you'll love every minute of it. Have you had a chance to look at the paper?"

He glanced at the folded paper on the table. "No, I haven't."

"Well, check out page one."

"Uh-oh. John, Jr.'s, handiwork?"

"Right. Actually, it's rather humorous."

Wes pushed the paper across the table. "You read it to me."

Jennifer opened the paper, and read:

*T'was Thanksgiving day and all
through the glen,
People were talking turkey, Tom or hen.
Tables were set, guests were arriving,
But one cook in town thought only about
surviving.*

Can't say I blame that cook, folks. He or she found a diamond necklace stuffed in the turkey, and the sheriff would like the owner to step forward. So best everybody take a look around. If you find one of your diamond necklaces missing, you know who to contact. It sounds like another mystery afoot to me, but I suppose that's to be expected in Calico. Meanwhile, let's hope the family who had that bright surprise waiting for them on Thanksgiving morning managed to enjoy their dinner, and that they plan on ordering a ham for Christmas.

Wes grinned. "Well, it could've been worse, I guess. Good thing he doesn't know about Roger."

"He might, before it's over. It's getting

late. We should be thinking about what we're going to have for dinner."

Wes walked to the refrigerator, opened the door, and closed it. "What would you say to having dinner at Kelly's, and then heading for the hospital?"

"I think it's a wonderful idea. If we leave within the hour, we can stop at the florist shop before it closes."

"I'd like to stop at the candy shop and the Mercantile too," Wes said, scribbling something at the bottom of the list.

Jennifer peeked over his shoulder and grinned. "Flowers, perfume, chocolates, and a pair of slippers, huh? You're going to spoil her, Grandfather."

Wes's cheeks flushed rosy pink. "You betcha. Should I wear my blue sweater or the green?"

"Wear your blue sweater, Grandfather. It's Emma's favorite."

Wes flushed again, and headed for the stairs.

Chapter Five

By four o'clock Monday afternoon, Jennifer and Ben were exhausted. The line of patients had been endless, making up for the slow days they'd had the week before. Most of the ailments had been intestinal disorders, which were directly related to the family pet receiving too much turkey and gravy, with a little cranberry sauce, pumpkin pie, and whipped cream tossed into the food bowl for good measure. At one point, Ben said he thought they should be handing out bottles of Alka-Seltzer along with their admonitions to the owners that Fido and Kitty would fare much better if they were kept on their regular diets, especially over the holidays.

It had also been a day filled with gossip and humor, as everybody tried to speculate who, among Calico's citizens, had been the recipient of the jewel-stuffed turkey. Jennifer wondered what they would say if they knew it had been the pastor's turkey, or if they would find it so amusing if they knew Roger Nessler's disappearance might be connected to the incident.

Now, with a half-hour break before their last appointment of the day arrived, Ben popped the top on a can of orange soda. "There isn't much point in your sticking around, Jennifer. I know you want to get to the hospital, and I can handle Fancy Dancer."

"Ah-ha, but can you handle Mrs. Thurman? She's almost as high-strung as her Maltese."

"That's because Judge Thurman pampers her as much as she pampers the dog, but don't worry. This isn't one of her exaggerated emergencies. The dog needs a shot, and I can deal with it."

Jennifer shrugged out of her lab coat, and tossed it in the laundry hamper. "So maybe you have some insight on how to deal with Emma? She's only been in the hospital two days, and she's having a fit. She says she feels claustrophobic, but I know it's because she's confined to a hospital bed while the town is in a frenzy, getting ready for Christmas."

"It's only the twenty-ninth of November." Ben chuckled. "Show her a calendar, and maybe she'll feel better."

"It would make her feel worse. Emma begins preparing for Christmas in August, has her shopping done by October, takes off the month of November for Thanksgiving, and then it's full steam ahead. With the exception of the tree, she likes to have the house decorated by the first of December, so she can concentrate on the baking and all the hoopla in general. She has every square on the calendar for the month of December marked with something, and now she's going to have to put it on hold. I don't think we've helped her mood, either. Grandfather couldn't find the crèche, the tree stand, or the cookie cutters, and we put the wrong lights on the little artificial tree in the foyer. She visualizes disaster at home, and feels helpless."

"But loved, I would imagine. Her hospital room looks like a florist shop. I stopped by yesterday, and couldn't find a spot to put the small plant Irene sent along. Irene has come down with her annual cold, so thought she'd better stay away. Happens every year. She gets through Thanksgiving, and then blooey."

"Well, she can commiserate with Emma, who insists she doesn't have time to be ill. Did you stop in and see Mrs. Masterson while you were in the hospital?"

"I did, and she was all smiles because she's going home today. Her family arrived from Scottsbluff, and tried to give Cracker a couple hundred dollars for boarding the horse, but he wouldn't take it. Told them to give it to us. I wouldn't take it, either. They were pretty insistent, so I told them to donate it to their favorite charity in our name, if it would make them feel better."

Jennifer smiled. "That was a nice thought, Ben. What about the disabled horse trailer?"

"They're hauling it off on a flatbed truck. They brought along another vehicle to tow the van, and a classy horse trailer, so Mr. Pippin will be riding home in style. It'll be quite a procession, though slow going because of the weather."

Jennifer looked out the window at the dark, angry clouds and sighed. "Emma is upset about the weather too. She thinks we're in for the worst winter in a decade, the town will come to a standstill, and she'll be stuck in the hospital until the spring thaw."

Ben grinned. "Well, you give her a kiss for me, and tell her not to worry. We'll get her home if we have to borrow Mr. Babkins' sled and pull it with a snowplow."

"I'll be sure and tell her. Give my best to Irene, and tell her to drink lots of tea and honey. Uh-oh. I hear a car out front. Must be Mrs. Thurman. Are you sure you can handle it alone?"

"Better than you can handle Emma. Now scoot!"

Jennifer headed for the back door with a smile on her face.

"I saw your cars in the parking lot, so I knew you were here," Jennifer said, walking into Emma's hospital room. She hugged her grandfather and Willy, and kissed Emma on both cheeks. "One of those kisses is from Ben, along with a message. He said no matter what the weather is like, we'll get you home if we have to borrow Mr. Babkins' sled, and pull it with a snowplow."

Emma rolled her eyes. "Now wouldn't that be the ticket. Though I wouldn't mind going on a sleigh ride when I'm feeling better. Haven't been on one of those in years. Last time was when I was about fifteen. Had a fancy for a tall, skinny young man with bright red hair. Can't even remember his name, but I remember getting stuck in a snowdrift and nearly freezing to death." She eyed Jennifer intently. "You look tired, Jennifer. Did you have a busy day?"

"We had an exhausting day treating an assortment of pets with intestinal problems because their owners stuffed them full of Thanksgiving goodies, and then we had to listen to everybody's theories regarding the diamond necklace."

"What are they saying?" Willy asked.

"They are more interested in who found the necklace than who put it in the turkey. I had to bite my tongue to keep from telling them. Has anybody talked to the sheriff today?"

"He called," Emma said. "Said he'd stop by on his way home. Said Ida is fixing a spaghetti dinner, so he won't be able to stay long." Her mouth turned down. "Spaghetti isn't one of my favorite dishes, but it would sure beat what they serve here. Your grand-daddy thinks he's fixed everything. He went and talked to somebody 'important' down-stairs, and set up a dinner for two. Can you beat that? He gets to eat right here with me, just like we were in a restaurant. Can't imagine why he would want to, when every-thing smells like disinfectant. And I don't care what they try to do to the food down in that kitchen. They aren't going to make it edible."

Wes winked at Jennifer. "I think she's go-ing to be pleasantly surprised. I would've or-dered for you too, but Willy has other plans."

Jennifer raised a brow. "Oh, really?"

Willy grinned. "If I buy you a hot dog at the mall, will you help me pick out a wel-come-home gift for my mother? I've always been terrible at that sort of thing, and I want it to be special."

"Sounds like bribery to me," Jennifer teased. "But I'll go with you, Willy. It sounds like fun."

Emma muttered, "One more thing for me

to worry about—the two of you out on that road in a snowstorm."

Jennifer reasoned, "It isn't snowing hard, Emma, and besides, Willy's 'boat' can get through anything."

Willy nodded. "That's why I bought that old souped-up Dodge from the county. It saw the sheriff through a lot of winters, and it's built like a tank."

"Speaking of cars, I think I need a new battery in mine," Wes said. "It's cranking over slower and slower, and this isn't the time of year for a car to conk out."

While Wes and Willy talked about cars, batteries, and prices, Jennifer sat down on the edge of the bed and took Emma's hand. "How are you feeling, Emma? And I'd like an honest answer."

Emma managed a smile. "When you look at me that way, I couldn't fib to you if I wanted to. I'm a bit sore, and it's hard to cough, but I feel a lot better than I did yesterday."

"Have they gotten you up much?"

"Off and on all day. I walk hunkered over like I'm one hundred and ten. The nurses keep telling me to straighten up, but it hurts. Guess the older you are, the harder it is to recuperate from something like this."

"It's hard for anybody to recuperate after major surgery, Emma. Did the doctor say when he's going to release you?"

"Thursday morning. I don't know if I can stand it for two more days. And when I think about everything I have to do at home . . ."

"You keep talking like that, and I'll tell the doctor to keep you here for a month!"

Emma puckered her lips. "You'd do that too, wouldn't you?"

"You bet I would. Everything is under control at home. Grandfather finally found the rest of the Christmas stuff, and most of the decorations are up, so all you have to do is get well. Promise me you won't give us any trouble?"

"I already promised Mr. Wes, so I suppose I can do the same for you. Don't want a relapse. I'd hate to be stuck here over Christmas!"

"Then be a good girl," Wes said, picking up the last of the conversation.

A few minutes later, the sheriff strode in, carrying a large stuffed brown bear. He handed it to Emma and gave her a hug.

"This is from Nettie. She has the sniffles, so she thought she'd better stay away."

Emma smiled delightedly. "How sweet! I haven't had a teddy bear since I was a youngster. Leave it to Nettie to think of something like this!"

A flush touched the sheriff's cheeks. "Yeah, well, she had an ulterior motive. She figured if you tell the bear all your troubles when you're alone, it might make it easier on your visitors."

"Uh-oh. She told you about her little visit yesterday, did she?"

"She did. Apparently she left here talking to herself."

Jennifer frowned. "Should I ask what happened?"

A sheepish grin tugged at the corners of Emma's mouth. "I got into a ruckus with one of my nurses while Nettie was here. She has a prune face, and a disposition to match, and we haven't gotten along from minute one. She wanted to fluff my pillow, and I wanted it flat. She wanted to open the drapes, and I wanted them closed. I won't tell you what happened after that."

The sheriff chuckled. "And my lips are sealed."

"Any takers on the necklace?" Willy asked the sheriff.

"A couple of crank calls, but that's about all. Nothing to report on Roger, either, and I backtracked it all the way to Lincoln."

"*If* he's from Lincoln," Willy said. "He might have been on the run when he arrived in Calico, and trouble followed him."

Jennifer took it one step further. "And maybe his name isn't really Roger Nessler."

Jim nodded. "Nothing on the police blotter in Lincoln, so that's a good possibility. I took fingerprints off his water glass in the hospital and shipped them off to state headquarters. Maybe that will help."

"What about the few months he's been in Calico?" Jennifer asked. "You know—did he make any friends, or have a social life?"

"Not according to Orris. Said he was on the shy side, and didn't make friends easily. About all he did for recreation was bowl. He wanted to join a bowling league, but didn't think he was good enough. That's it."

"Did you poke around the bowling alley?" Wes asked.

"I did. A few people knew who he was, but didn't know him personally. Jake Barnette said he tried to talk Roger into taking lessons to better his game, but the kid couldn't afford it."

"Jake Barnette?" Jennifer asked. "The name isn't familiar."

"Barnette owns Cottonwood Lanes, Jennifer. He owned a western boot shop in Lincoln for years, until he retired and decided to build his dream."

"The bowling alley?"

"Uh-huh. Guess that was about three years ago. The bowling alley is his life now, and that's the way he wants it. He isn't married, so it's his call all the way. He also built a house along Cottonwood Creek, and I hear it's quite a showplace."

"Why did he settle in Calico?"

"Two reasons. Property was reasonable, and he saw it as a town with a future."

Wes mumbled, "It might be a town with a future, but it's still getting too big for its britches. Guess he must have been happy when the mall and all those apartment complexes went up."

"Well, it brought in business, that's for sure. He's doing okay. Unfortunately, he wasn't much help as far as Roger was concerned, other than to corroborate Orris's story about Roger being on the shy side, and a loner. I went out there expecting just what I got—zero. Zip."

Emma asked, "Did you tell the people at the bowling alley that Roger left the hospital under mysterious circumstances?"

"In so many words, and all I got was a 'what's-the-big-deal' reaction. I have the feeling I'm gonna end up with an unsolved mystery on my hands, and boy, do I hate that! And poor Orris is walking around in a daze. He keeps saying Roger's head injury must have been more serious than they thought, and that's why he wandered off. I told him it wasn't likely he could walk around town in a hospital gown and a bandage on his head, and go unnoticed. There was one thing, though. Orris said a man came into the market asking for Roger the day of the accident, while Roger was delivering the turkey to the Butler farm. The man said he'd wait. Orris didn't see him again until just before closing time. By then, Orris had gotten the call about the accident. When he told the man Roger was in the hospital, the man stalked off in a huff."

"Did Orris know him?" Willy asked.

"Nope. He'd never seen him before."

"What about a description?"

"Uh-huh. I got that. Short, thin, dark hair and eyes, and he was wearing a tan jacket."

"Could be the other half of the puzzle," Wes said.

"Yeah. The guy could be the trouble that followed Roger, if that's his name, from Lincoln, if that's where he's from. Now all I have to do is find the man, and maybe I'll find Roger, but it isn't going to be easy. Other than Orris, nobody at the market noticed the stranger."

"So now what?" Willy asked.

"I keep poking around, and hope I get a break." He looked at his watch. "Gotta go. Ida said dinner is at six, and I'm trying to keep from creating waves. If any emergencies pop up tonight, my deputies are gonna have to handle them."

Jennifer didn't want to create waves either, so she kept her thoughts to herself, though Willy kept watching her out of the corner of his eye.

A few minutes later, Jennifer hugged Emma and her grandfather and said they had better get going too, because she didn't want to get home late. She literally dragged Willy out the door.

Willy waited until they were in the elevator before he said, "Okay, Jenny. Out with it."

She smiled up at him. "I never could fool you, could I? Would you mind if we stop at the bowling alley on our way to the mall?"

Willy sighed. "I had the feeling it might be something like that. You think Jim missed something?"

"Maybe, or maybe it's just this feeling I can't seem to shake. I wanted to ask the sheriff who he talked to at the bowling alley, other than the owner, but I knew if I did, I'd be sending up a red flag. Just the fact we're driving to the mall in this weather has Emma worried enough."

"Okay, so you didn't want to worry Emma or your grandfather. I can understand that, but what would be the point in going to the bowling alley?" He sighed. "I know, you think the sheriff missed something, and I guess I'd be foolish to doubt your instincts. We might as well save some time and eat there, if you're up to a greasy hamburger and fries."

"Surely they must have something else on the menu."

"Of course. Greasy hot dogs and greasy chili."

Jennifer cringed as the elevator door swooshed open, and they headed outside.

Chapter Six

It wasn't quite six o'clock when Jennifer and Willy walked into the bowling alley and took a table on the elevated concourse overlooking the lanes. There were twenty of them spread across the floor of the cavernous building, reminding Jennifer of tall, flat tree trunks, with bowling pins for branches. Only half of them were in use, mostly by couples and families. One man down at the far end handled the ball like a professional.

"Want to bowl a couple of games before we eat?" Willy asked.

Jennifer shook her head vigorously. "I've only been bowling once in my life, and the experience left me wondering how bowlers survive. I literally wore my thumb raw."

"Was that while you were in college?"

"Vet school. One of the guys in our group had a bottle of collodion, a vile-smelling stuff that's a mixture of pyroxylin and ether, and painted my thumb. It was supposed to protect it from further damage, but it didn't stop it from hurting. I'm sure bowling is a nice, healthy sport, but I'd much rather go horseback riding, hiking, or play a game of tennis. I like to ice-skate in the winter, and— Here comes the waitress, and she isn't carrying a menu."

Willy grinned. "I told you. Greasy hamburgers, hot dogs, and chili. Who needs a menu for that?"

"The special tonight is beef potpie," the perky, dark-haired waitress said with a smile. "Other than that, about all we have to offer is hamburgers, hot dogs, and chili."

"I'll have the potpie," Jennifer said.

Willy winked at Jennifer. "I'll have a hamburger."

"Have you been working here long?" Jennifer asked while the waitress took down the order.

"Since it opened, though the boss keeps

changing my hours. Wish he'd make up his mind. The best nights to work are when the leagues bowl. Lots of tips."

"Then I would imagine you know most of the regulars?"

"Most of them."

"What about Roger Nessler?"

The waitress stiffened. "Can't help you. I know who he is, but I don't really *know* him, if you know what I mean. The sheriff was in, asking questions earlier. I was sorry to hear Roger was in a car accident, but as far as his disappearance, if that's what it was . . . umm, well . . ."

Jennifer said, "We were told he bowls here a lot."

"I-I guess. But he wasn't very good at it."

"Did he bowl alone?"

"Yeah, he did. I felt kinda sorry for him because—" She bit at her lip. "I'd better get your order in before the place starts to fill up."

"Just one more question," Willy said. "Is there anybody else around that might be able to answer our questions without getting a case of the nervous jitters?"

High color swept the waitress's cheeks.

"N-no . . . No, not really. See, the boss says stuff like this is bad for business."

"Stuff like this?" Willy asked.

"Yeah, you know. The cops hanging out and asking questions."

"Is your boss the tall, dark man in the sport coat who's talking to the desk clerk?"

"Yeah. Mr. Barnette. He's a nice man, and he's been a good boss. I-I don't want to lose my job."

Jennifer noted the name tag on the waitress's white blouse. "I can understand your loyalty, Penny, but this is really important. Roger was injured in the accident, and he belongs in the hospital."

"I'm sorry, but I can't help you," Penny mumbled, and then hurried off.

Jennifer sighed. "She's holding out on us, Willy."

"Might be because the boss was staring holes through her. Shall we create a few more nervous stomachs, and circulate?"

Jennifer nodded. "Supposedly, Roger bowled alone, so let's start with the man down at the end lane. A loner might know another loner."

Jennifer and Willy walked down the carpeted concourse until they were behind the single bowler, but waited until he'd returned to the score table to mark a frame before they headed down the stairs. He was a giant of a man with blond spiky hair and a leather-like face, and when he looked up, he wasn't smiling.

"Hi," Jennifer said.

His reply was gruff. "If you're gonna use the lane next door, I'd better tell ya I don't like nobody talkin' when I'm bowlin'. That's why I always get this lane. Nobody wants to bowl wedged up against the wall, and nobody wants to bowl next to me."

Jennifer gave the man her brightest smile. "Don't worry, sir. We're not going to bowl. We just want to ask you a few questions."

Bushy brows furrowed over steel-gray eyes. "Yeah? About what?"

"We're trying to locate Roger Nessler, and we were told he bowls here all the time."

Muscles worked along his thick jawline. "Monday, Wednesday, and Friday nights. Same nights Tracy works, only she ain't here tonight. Called in sick."

"Is Tracy his girlfriend?"

"He'd like to think so. I can tell ya right

now old Roger is a jerk." He looked at Willy. "You a cop?"

Willy said, "No, I'm not a cop. Why?"

The man shrugged. "The sheriff was in here earlier, digging around. Figured he'd be back. Look, if you ain't a cop, I ain't sayin' boo. Now, if ya don't mind, I got a game to finish."

"Friendly sort," Willy said after they were out of earshot. "Now what?"

"Why waste time? Let's talk to the boss. He's been watching us since Penny took our order, and he doesn't look happy."

Willy nodded. "You talk to him, and I'll talk to the desk clerk. Sooner or later, somebody is going to give us something we can work with."

Jennifer approached Jake Barnette, who was now leaning against the wall near the bar, and tried for a smile again. "Excuse me, but—"

He cut her off. "You know Deke?"

"Deke?"

"You and your friend were just talking to him, lady."

"No, we don't know him, but we were hoping he could give us some information about a friend of ours. He was in an auto accident a few days ago, and seems to have disappeared."

"Roger Nessler. I already answered the sheriff's questions."

"And I'm sorry to have to bother you again, Mr. Barnette, but—"

"I suppose Penny gave you my name and pointed me out?"

"The sheriff gave us your name, Mr. Barnette. Penny simply verified the fact that you're the boss."

"Well, I'll tell you what I told the sheriff. I'm sorry the Nessler kid was in an accident, but I don't much care if he drops off the face of the earth. He would tie up a lane for hours bowling one game, and then get huffy when I asked him to hurry up because people were waiting in line. Business is business. If you don't look out for number one, nobody will. And you are?"

"A concerned friend. Apparently Deke isn't too fond of Roger, either."

"Deke is a good bowler and takes the game seriously, which is a lot more than I say for Roger. I tried to get him to take lessons, but he said he couldn't afford it. Now, if you'll excuse me, it looks like your friend is giving Pete a bad time."

Jennifer followed Jake Barnette to the desk, and listened to the desk clerk's angry words.

"I told this guy I don't know Roger Nessler, Mr. Barnette, but he won't take no for an answer."

"You aren't the police," Barnette said to Willy and Jennifer. "So I suggest you return to your dinner."

Willy muttered, "I'm not going to ask any more questions, so you can both relax."

Jennifer waited until they were seated at their table again before she said, "Is it my imagination, or is everybody acting strange?"

"I was thinking more like 'weird,' " Willy muttered. "They all know more than they're telling us, Jenny. Here comes our waitress. Shall we grill her again?"

Jennifer grinned. "I have a better idea. Play along?"

"You lead the way."

Jennifer smiled up at the waitress as she placed their food on the table. "We had a little chat with Deke and your boss, Penny, and they told us Roger was interested in a waitress named Tracy. Was she interested in him?"

Deke had finished bowling and was on the concourse now, glaring at Penny. Penny glanced over her shoulder and lowered her voice. "Gee, I don't know . . . Well, if the boss told you about it . . . Th-they were dating, but sort of cooled things when they were here because of Deke."

"Why was that?" Willy asked.

"Because Deke liked her too, and was always causing problems."

"Like picking fights with Roger?"

"Yeah, only Roger wouldn't fight him, because he knew Deke could snap him like a twig. Well, look at him. He's built like Godzilla."

"Was Tracy dating Deke before Roger came to town?"

"No, and that's what made her so mad. Deke had no right to act that way. For sure, he didn't have the right to tell her who she could or couldn't date. She fell for Roger right off. At first, she said she felt sorry for him because he wanted to bowl better and couldn't. Well, he could, but he wasn't very good at it, if you know what I mean. But then later, she told me the way she felt about him didn't have anything to do with sympathy. She really liked him for who he was."

"And who was that?" Jennifer asked.

"A shy guy who had a heart as big as the ocean. He kept telling her he was about to come into some big money, and that she'd better start packing, because he was going to take her away from Calico, and build her a big house somewhere along the Missouri River."

Jennifer exchanged glances with Willy. "Did she believe him?"

"No, but she went along with his fantasy. I probably shouldn't be telling you this, but . . ."

Jennifer said, "You can speak freely, Penny. We're trying to help Roger, and all we want is a little cooperation."

Willy asked, "Have you talked to Tracy since Roger disappeared from the hospital?"

Penny shook her head. "To tell you the truth, I kinda figured she was with Roger. Just a feeling, you know?"

"I know all about feelings," Jennifer replied. "Do you know where Tracy lives?"

Penny looked over her shoulder again, but Deke was gone. She sighed with relief.

"She said something about an apartment, but never mentioned the address."

Willy said, "Your boss must have her address."

"Sure he does, but he won't give it to you. It's his policy to protect his employees, if you know what I mean. Deke tried to get it out of him one time, and I thought they were going to come to blows. I've got to get back to work. Sorry I couldn't be more help."

After Penny moved off to another table, Willy said, "About all we can do now is pass the info on to the sheriff in the morning, and let him handle it. He can get Tracy's address from Barnette easily enough. So, do you think Roger is with Tracy?"

"I do. And I think she's the one who helped him sneak out of the hospital. Now all we have to do is find out why."

"I think the answer is obvious. Roger is hiding out because he's afraid of somebody. The big question is, who?"

"Deke?"

"Maybe, but we can't overlook the stranger at the butcher shop. Maybe the stranger was the one who was supposed to get the necklace, and for some reason, Roger didn't want to give it to him."

"So he stuffed the necklace in a turkey to hide it? I don't know, Willy. None of it makes any sense. Roger told Tracy he was coming into a lot of money, and that had to be the money he expected to get for the necklace." She looked down at the greasy meat and vegetables swimming around under a soggy crust, and groaned. "I've lost my appetite."

Willy studied the hamburger in front of him for a few moments, and reached in his pocket. "Ten bucks ought to cover the meal and the tip," he said, tossing the bill on the table. "A hot dog in the mall sounds pretty good about now."

Jennifer nodded. She was eager to get away from the smell of greasy food, the sound of clattering bowling pins, and a feeling of apprehension. She struggled to her feet, and muttered, "Let's get out of here, Willy."

Willy waited until they were in his car with the doors locked before he said, "You felt like we were sitting on top of all the answers too, didn't you?"

Jennifer pulled a woolen lap robe over her legs and shivered. "Yes I did, and I felt sort of scared for some reason."

Willy started the car. "One perfectly normal mall coming up. If you behave, I'll even take you to see Santa."

Jennifer reached over and squeezed his hand.

It was almost nine when they left the mall. They'd found a book of poetry for Willy's mother early on, but had taken their time browsing through the stores, listening to carolers, and eating hot dogs at the little stand near the bookstore. But more important, they had shared a couple of hours without having to worry about anything, and the mood was light as Willy carefully maneuvered the Dodge along the slick highway toward town.

Until Willy said, "Somebody is following us, Jenny."

Jennifer turned around, and although she could see the headlights through the falling snow, she couldn't see the vehicle. "Th-this is a well-traveled road, Willy, and it's snowing. It's impossible to see the car."

"I know, but it wasn't snowing when we left the bowling alley. I saw a black truck pull out a few seconds behind us."

"And?" Jennifer asked, barely above a whispered breath.

"It followed us to the mall, and now it's following us again."

"Did you see it in the mall parking lot?"

"I did. I didn't want to frighten you. It was parked under a tree near the south entrance."

"Deke?"

"That would be my guess. He left the bowling alley before we did, and could have been waiting for us in his truck."

"Maybe it's a coincidence."

"Maybe. I have a way to find out, if you're game."

Jennifer felt a chill, and hugged the lap robe close. "How?"

"We're coming up on Marshton Road. About a mile in is the turnoff to the Cramer farm. It's a dead end, Jenny. He wouldn't follow us unless he's . . ."

"Following us," she whispered. "What happens if he does?"

"If the Cramers are home, we'll stop and call the sheriff. If they aren't, we'll keep going. There's an old road on the back side of the property that will eventually bring us out on River Road near the high school. I discovered it one day when I was seventeen and painting their house. Ned Cramer said he used it in the old days as an escape route to get away from the outlaws. He was teasing, but I was just a kid, and believed him."

"That's right, you were just a kid, Willy. I remember that summer you painted houses for extra money. That was a long time ago. Maybe the road is gone, or it's overgrown by now, and we won't be able to get through."

"We'll get through, Jenny, and that's a promise. Are you with me?"

"Yes, but . . . If it is Deke, why is he following us?"

Willy sighed. "I wish I knew."

There was another part to that question, but Jennifer kept it to herself. What was Deke going to do if he caught them? Or worse, what if it wasn't Deke at all? What if it was the short, thin stranger in the tan jacket?

Jennifer double-checked her seat belt, and gritted her teeth, bracing herself for what promised to be a hair-raising ride. The situation had suddenly turned ominous. A few days ago, there had been another mystery to solve, and it had seemed exciting. Now it didn't seem exciting at all.

* * *

It had stopped snowing by the time they reached the turnoff to the Cramer farm, but the wind was up, blowing drifts across the road. If it hadn't been for the mailbox, Willy would have missed the turn. Now, as he gripped the wheel and tried to keep the vehicle parallel with the trees on either side of the private road, Jennifer turned around in her seat and waited for their pursuer, who hadn't been more than a few seconds behind them from the time they turned onto Marshton Road.

"Maybe he'll drive on," she said. "Even bad guys have brains. He has to know following us into a place like this would be crazy!"

"I don't know, Jenny. I got a good look at the truck when we were at the mall. Dark, tinted windows, no tailgate, and a roll bar. Old Betsy here is built like a tank, but that truck is a tank. And don't forget, he probably doesn't know we're on a dead-end road."

"How much further to the house?"

"About a quarter of a mile. We should see the lights through the trees in a few minutes."

"*If* the Cramers are home."

"They have to be in their sixties now, Jenny. I don't think they'd venture out on a night like this."

"But with the mall so close to them now, and all those sales—" Jennifer's breath caught in her throat, as headlights lit up the night behind them. "He's right behind us, Willy!"

"Looks like we have our answer," Willy muttered. "Hang on. The lights are on in the house, and I'm going to try for a little more speed."

A dozen things flashed through Jennifer's mind all in a matter of seconds while she hung on and said a quick prayer. The Cramers could have turned on the lights before they left the house. One miscalculation on Willy's part, and they would get bogged down in the snow. The black truck seemed to be gaining on them. Did their pursuer have a weapon? What if the Cramers were home, but the phone lines were down? What if the Cramers didn't have a phone?

Willy pulled up in front of the house and cut the engine. Before Jennifer could gather her thoughts, he was on the passenger side of the vehicle, and had the door open. "Come on!" he exclaimed, grabbing her hand. "We have just enough time to get into the house!"

And then what? Jennifer wanted to scream at him, but saved her energy for the trek through the snow.

By the time they'd reached the porch, the truck had entered the far side of the clearing. Willy banged on the door, and yelled, "Ned, are you in there?"

Seconds later, though it seemed like an eternity, Ned Cramer opened the door, and they hurried inside.

Mrs. Cramer was standing in the middle of the living room, and her eyes were huge in her pale face. "Willy? Jennifer? What on earth . . ."

Trying to keep his wits about him, and his voice under control, Willy said, "I'll explain in a minute. Are all the doors and windows locked?"

Ned Cramer locked the front door, and nodded. "They are now."

"Good. Is your shotgun handy?"

"It's in the bedroom . . ."

"Get it, and make sure it's loaded." Willy pulled the lacy curtains apart, and shook his head. "I can't see anything. If he's out there, he's turned off the headlights."

"He's out there," Jennifer said. "Listen. You can hear the engine."

Willy grunted. "This guy has nerve."

Mrs. Cramer, who was wearing a blue chenille bathrobe and had her white hair in rollers, dropped to the nearest chair and clasped her hands in her lap. "Dear, oh dear, what on earth is going on?"

"Well, whatever it is, it ain't good," Ned Cramer said, returning with the shotgun. "Have we got us an outlaw, boy?"

The older man's comment brought a smile to Willy's face. "We got us an outlaw, Ned, so you just keep that gun aimed at the door."

Jennifer listened to the truck engine fade in the distance, and took a deep breath. "He's leaving."

Willy held up his hand for silence, and then nodded. "Well, it looks like we won this round." He smiled at the Cramers. "Sorry to burst in on you like this, but it was about all we could do, under the circumstances."

Ned removed the shell, placed the shotgun over his shoulder, and gave Willy a toothless grin. "And it's them circumstances I want to hear all about. Martha has the hot water ready for tea, so we can sit a spell by the fire and talk, while you thaw out."

"I want to call the sheriff first," Willy said.

The man nodded. "The phone is in the kitchen. Help yourself."

Jennifer had never been in the Cramer house, but they were members of the church, and Martha was good friends with Emma. She knew them to be kind people who had raised five children in the weathered old farmhouse filled with antiques. Love and warmth filled every corner.

Jennifer was admiring the assortment of framed photographs on the mantel when Willy walked in. His face was grim. "The sheriff says he can't do much without the license plate number, but he'll call in the description of the truck to his deputies. He'll also send a deputy out first thing in the morning to take a look around, but he's afraid the wind and snow will wipe out any evidence, like the tire tracks."

"Did you tell him about Deke?"

"I did. He isn't familiar with the name, but he'll talk to Barnette, and hopefully get some answers, along with Tracy's address."

Ned shook his head. "So many new names in town, nobody knows anybody anymore."

"Hardly see a familiar face in town, either, and it's sad," Martha said, carrying in a teapot and cups on a tray. "Now suppose you tell us what this is all about."

They were working on a second cup of tea by the time Willy finished telling them the story. Hearing it like that, from start to finish, left Jennifer shaking her head right along with the Cramers. The whole thing seemed preposterous!

Ned wiped a hand over the stubble of beard on his chin. "I can't offer much in the way of advice, one way or the other, except maybe about the last part of your story. Might be the same thing that happened to me, years ago when I was in my twenties. I was living in San Francisco, and had me an old Ford. I was on my way home that night, and the fog was coming in thick off the water. Couldn't see a thing but the taillights of the vehicle in front of me. I figured I'd let the driver lead the way, and kept my fingers crossed that he knew where he was going. He did, and I ended up following him right into his driveway. It snowed pretty good out there tonight. Hard to see the lines on the road. Maybe he was following you, hoping you knew where you was going."

"I'm sure that's it," Martha said, managing a smile. But Jennifer could see the wariness in her brown eyes. It hadn't snowed *that* hard. Nor had it been snowing when they left the bowling alley.

Ned bobbed his head. "I'm sure that's it. Best thing now is to make sure you get back to town safe and sound. Think you should take my 'getaway' road. That'll bring you out near the high school." He grinned at Jennifer. "Used to use that road when the outlaws was after me."

Martha scowled. "Don't listen to him, Jennifer. He uses it all the time as a shortcut to town, and that's the only reason he put it in. Anything to save gasoline and time. It winds around a bit, but it's as good as any of our county roads, and probably in better condition. Speaking of conditions, how is Emma doing? I had some flowers delivered to the hospital."

"She's feeling much better, Martha, and can't wait to get home."

"Well, you give her our best. And you tell your granddaddy we'll be in church on Sunday, unless we get snowed in."

Ned snorted. "That's why we got the snowplow, Martha. You tell me a time when we've been snowed in?"

"There's always a first time," Martha returned.

Willy got to his feet. "Thanks for the tea, and the hospitality, but we'd better be going."

Martha nodded. "Well, you two come back again, you hear?"

Jennifer shook hands warmly with the Cramers, and followed Willy out into the bitter cold, trying to swallow around the tightness in her throat. She didn't want to leave the warmth of their home, and the security she'd felt behind locked doors. Had the driver of the black truck given up the pursuit? Or was he parked on Marshton Road, waiting?

Suddenly very glad they were taking the back road to town, Jennifer climbed in the Dodge, wrapped up in the lap robe, and closed her eyes.

"We have to stop at the hospital and get your Jeep," Willy said, climbing in beside her. He leaned over and kissed her cheek. "You must be exhausted, Jenny."

Jennifer felt herself drifting off, but managed to say, "Sleepy, too . . ."

* * *

"We're at the hospital, Jenny . . ."

Jennifer awoke to a gentle nudge and Willy's words, and shook her head to clear it. "S-sorry. I didn't mean to fall asleep."

Willy chuckled. "Must mean you trust my driving."

Jennifer shrugged out of the lap robe. "Were we . . ."

"Followed? No, we weren't, so the ordeal is over, at least for now. Hmm, Wes is still here."

Jennifer looked at her grandfather's snow-covered sedan, and frowned. "That's strange. It's after visiting hours."

"Maybe he couldn't get the car started."

Jennifer watched her grandfather walk out of the building, and smiled. "Or he's been waiting for us. Here he comes."

"Are you going to tell him about the truck?"

"I'd rather not, but he'll know something is wrong by the expression on my face, and he won't rest until he has all the answers. But I think I'll wait until we're home."

"Well, hello, you two," Wes said, trudging the final few feet through the snow. He shook Willy's hand. "Thanks for bringing

Jennifer back safe and sound. Nasty weather. We've been a little concerned."

Willy smiled. "I told you the Dodge can plow through anything. I'll call you tomorrow, Jenny."

Wes waited until Willy had driven off, and then gave Jennifer a sheepish grin. "I knew you'd be picking up your Jeep sooner or later, so thought I'd stick around. Emma thought it was a good idea too." He pointed up. "If you give her a wave, she'll get away from that blamed window and go to bed."

Jennifer looked up where Emma was outlined against the light in her third-story window, and waved. "Is she okay?"

Wes's eyes narrowed over Jennifer. "She's fine, sweetheart, but I'm not so sure about you. I know *that* look."

Jennifer sighed. "Come on, Grandfather. Let's go home and fix some hot chocolate, and I'll tell you all about it."

"I noticed a few stars popping out between the clouds on the way home, so I'd say the storm has finally moved on," Wes said, pouring the rest of the hot chocolate in their cups.

"And you're avoiding my question," Jennifer said with a scowl. "I told you every single detail about our little ordeal, and yet you won't give me a simple yes or no. So I'll ask you again. Did Emma enjoy the special dinner you arranged at the hospital?"

Wes sat down at the table and sighed. "No, she didn't, and for that I'm truly sorry. But it wasn't Emma's fault. I mean, she wasn't being difficult. The food just wasn't good, that's all. It took me a while to figure it out, and I finally decided it was too bland. No taste. Guess that's to be expected in a hospital, but I sure did want to put a smile on her face."

"She smiled when Sheriff Cody gave her the stuffed bear."

"Uh-huh, and that's the kind of smile I wanted to see."

"She'll smile when she's finally home, Grandfather. She hates it in the hospital, and I can't blame her. She's a vital woman, and needs to be going and doing to be happy."

"Along with taking care of us. Are you going to tell her about what you're calling 'your little ordeal'?"

"Do you think I should?"

"I don't think she should be told anything that might worry her."

"Don't you suppose she'll guess something's wrong?"

"Not unless you give her a reason."

"Is that your subtle way of telling me to stay out of it?"

Wes shrugged. "You have to do what you have to do, sweetheart, but if you want my opinion, I think the sheriff should take it from here. I see it as one big dilemma with Roger and the diamond necklace in the middle, and I think what earlier was just a mystery has now become a dangerous situation."

She gave him a weary smile. "Don't worry. I plan to stay out of it, and I'm sure Willy feels the same way."

He patted her hand. "I'm glad, because I sure need your undivided attention on the home front. We have two days before Emma comes home, and I want everything to be perfect."

"Emma wanted everything to be perfect for Thanksgiving too, and I'll tell you what I told her. It doesn't have to be perfect, as long as we're together."

"Right. Well, best you remember that

when she walks through the door and finds everything she loves out of whack. Like the little porcelain bird on the table beside her reading chair. Does it sit to the right or the left of the candy dish? Oh, and here's a good one, if you want a genuine dilemma. She wants to wear her new flowered dress home from the hospital. She has a closet full of flowered dresses, and they all look new to me."

"I know which one she's talking about, Grandfather, so relax!"

"Then best we get it out of the closet right now, so I don't get into a muddle on Thursday morning. Boy, oh boy, I wouldn't want that!"

Jennifer followed her grandfather into Emma's bedroom, trying to hold back the smile. She loved him with all her heart, and for the first time, she realized how much he loved Emma.

Chapter Seven

On Tuesday morning, Jennifer awoke to a thick blanket of fog that obscured everything outside her bedroom window but the vague outline of the nearest trees. It happened sometimes after a storm, because of Calico's proximity to the river, but it was never welcome. And if it got worse, it could bring the town to a virtual standstill.

Jennifer showered and dressed, and went downstairs. She knew her grandfather was up, because she could smell freshly brewed coffee, but she wasn't prepared for the somber expression on his face. For a moment she thought Emma had taken a turn for the worse, until he said, "It's bad, sweetheart. I listened to the six-o'clock news, and it looks like this is only the beginning. Without a breeze to stir things up, and the cold temperatures, the moisture on the ground is freezing into sheets of ice, and the roads are already too slick to travel. They're suggesting everybody stay home today, but you know a lot of folks won't, and that's what worries me. The last time we had fog this thick, we had a ten-car pileup on Route 5, and too many fender benders around town to count."

"I'd better call Ben," Jennifer said, pouring herself a cup of coffee.

"He called after the newscast, and said unless there's an emergency, he'll see you tomorrow, *if* the fog lifts."

"Did he say anything about Irene?"

Wes pulled a saucepan out of the cupboard and filled it with water. "He did. She's feeling so poorly, she can hardly get her head off the pillow, so he was planning to stay home today anyway. This is an oatmeal morning, Jennifer. Join me?"

"Oatmeal sounds yummy. This is a good cookie baking morning too, Grandfather. Emma has most of the ingredients on hand."

Wes shook his head. "Emma. She's going to have a fit. She was so worried about getting stuck in the hospital because of the snowstorm, and now this. We'd better not tell her we're baking cookies in her cozy kitchen, or it'll make her feel worse."

"Would you rather wait until she comes home to bake cookies?"

Wes nodded. "I know, you probably think it's silly of me, but . . ."

"I don't think it's silly at all, and I understand."

Wes held up the box of oatmeal. "Well, I guess it wouldn't hurt to make a batch of oatmeal cookies. Can't really call it Christmas baking, then." He gave her a sly smile. "Maybe if we use up all the raisins, Emma won't be able to make the fruitcake."

Jennifer grinned. When it came to fruitcake, they were a house divided, even though Emma kept insisting that someday Wes was going to acquire a taste for it. Whenever he could, he'd cut a slice and take it out to the birds, proclaiming Johnny Carson was right—there was only one fruitcake in the whole world, and year after year, it kept finding its way back to his house.

For the rest of the morning, they baked

oatmeal cookies, took turns talking to Emma on the phone, who kept calling with updates on the weather, and listened to a tape of Christmas carols, hoping it would put them in a festive mood. But they both knew better. The true Christmas spirit wouldn't begin until Emma walked through the door.

They were eating lunch when Willy called. He'd talked to the sheriff, but there wasn't anything to report. The fog had caused so many problems, he hadn't had a chance to get to the bowling alley, or send a deputy out to the Cramers'. Willy said the sheriff hadn't seemed too concerned, and the Roger Nessler situation didn't seem to be one of his top priorities. As far as the car that had followed them onto the Cramer property was concerned, the sheriff was convinced it had been some poor soul who had been lost in the storm. It left Jennifer with a strange feeling of regret, like she'd suddenly lost the last chapter in a book, and would never know the ending. Even worse was the sick feeling she had deep inside of her that she couldn't seem to shake, no matter how hard she tried. Roger Nessler was in danger, his time was running out, and nobody was going to do anything about it.

And then a little after two, the fog lifted, and the mood brightened. Emma had already said she didn't want them driving to the hospital, no matter what, but they were considering it anyway. Then Ben called. The clinic had an emergency. Fancy Dancer couldn't breathe, Mr. Thurman had the car, and Mrs. Thurman was hysterical because there was no way to get the dog to the clinic. Ben couldn't leave Irene, so it was up to Jennifer to make the house call.

Jennifer explained the situation to Wes while she pulled on her boots, but all she got in return was a scowl. "The Thurmans live out on River Road, sweetheart. The fog might be even thicker out there, so there is no way I'm going to let you go alone."

Jennifer sighed. "This whole thing might be a complete waste of time, Grandfather. Mrs. Thurman throws a tizzy if Fancy Dancer sneezes."

"Uh-huh, well, you know what they say about crying wolf."

"I know, and that's why I can't ignore the call. I'd never forgive myself if something was really wrong with the pooch, or with

Mrs. Thurman, for that matter. Ben said she was hysterical."

"Barbara Thurman is always hysterical about something," Wes said, shrugging into his parka. "If the weather holds, we can stop by and see Emma on our way home."

Jennifer glanced at the clock on the wall. It would be dark in less than three hours. "What if Emma calls while we're gone?"

"She won't. She said she's watching "Oprah" at three and "Jenny Jones" at four, and she'll be getting her dinner tray at five. We're safe, at least until then."

Jennifer smiled, and headed for the door.

Jennifer decided after only a few miles that it was a very strange day. There were sections of town that were dazzling bright in sunlight, sections that were bogged down under pea-soup fog, and sections that were in between, where the sun and fog mingled together in an eerie glow. Driving along River Road gave them a little bit of all of it, with the emphasis on pea soup. Wes kept quiet, but Jennifer knew what he was thinking. This was madness, and if they didn't get back to town before dark, they might not get back at all.

Jennifer was so intent on the road, she didn't see the slow-moving vehicle in front of them until it was simply there, looming dark and shadowy. She hit the brakes, and then gasped. "Oh, my goodness, I think it's the black truck!"

Instantly alert, Wes leaned forward, peering through the windshield. "Are you sure?"

She backed off a little, and nodded. "I'm sure. All I saw last night were the headlights, but Willy described it, Grandfather. Dark tinted windows, a roll bar, and a missing tailgate . . . The driver won't recognize the Jeep, but if it's Deke, he'll recognize me."

"We're not likely to get close enough for that, Jennifer."

"Can you see the license plate number?"

"Sure can."

"Get the notebook and pen out of my purse— Oh, no, he's speeding up!" Within seconds, the truck had disappeared in the fog.

"That's one crazy driver," Wes muttered.

"Do you suppose he lives around here?"

Wes made a verbal list. "We've got three farms, the Grange, the high school, a couple of houses, the Thurman place, the Circle Q

Ranch, and the two cottages tucked in at the corner of Marshton and River Road. Not much beyond that."

"And we have Willy's neighborhood on the back side of the high school," Jennifer said with a shudder. "Just the thought of that crazy person living near Willy . . ."

"Willy knows his neighbors, so it isn't likely. I'd say he's long gone, so best we concentrate on where we're going. We don't want to miss the Thurman driveway."

Jennifer kept her eyes riveted on the road, but her thoughts were on the black truck and the unknown driver. The sheriff thought the driver had followed them last night because he was lost in the snowstorm. But driving through dense fog was much worse, and the truck had sped away with ease. Jennifer believed that, like last night, the driver knew exactly what he was doing.

The fog had lifted a little by the time they reached the Thurmans' sprawling ranch house, and Jennifer wasn't surprised to see Mrs. Thurman standing out front, shivering from the cold. She was a tall, handsome woman with dark, wavy hair, and her expressive brown eyes were full of tears. The first words out of her mouth were "I-I think he's dying!" And then, "He was playing with his little rubber ball, and all of a sudden he couldn't breathe!"

Wes put a comforting arm around the woman's shoulders. "You shouldn't be out here without a wrap, Barbara. Let's go in the house . . ."

"I can't! I think he's dying!"

"Where is he?" Jennifer asked.

"In the kitchen. You go through the living room, and down a little hallway . . . Well, you know that. You've been here before, or have you? I don't know what I'd do if he died . . ."

Jennifer left Wes to deal with Mrs. Thurman, and hurried into the house. It took only a moment to find Fancy Dancer in the kitchen, and it took even less time to assess what had happened. The dog had of course swallowed the little rubber ball, and it was lodged in his throat.

The dog was making ragged gasping noises as it tried to suck in air, and looked up at Jennifer with pleading, sorrowful brown eyes.

"Take it easy, fella," Jennifer said, reaching down his throat. "That's it. Don't fight . . . Ah, there it is." She extracted the ball, checked the dog's vital signs, and smiled. He was going to be just fine, as long as he was kept away from small balls and other objects he might try to ingest. She picked him up and hugged him close. "Come on, little fella. Let's go find your 'mommy' and tell her how she can prevent this from happening again."

Barbara Thurman and Wes were still outside, and the reunion was about what Jennifer expected. The dog barked, the woman wept, and chaos prevailed. "He's very lucky," Jennifer said, when she could finally get Mrs. Thurman's attention. "If the ball had been smaller, it could have lodged further down, necessitating surgery. Or, if it had been a little larger, it could have totally blocked off his windpipe. You have a small dog, so think big when you give him balls or toys. Just like having a small child. If he has trouble getting it into his mouth, consider it safe."

Barbara Thurman cast her eyes downward. "I don't know what to say, except thanks."

"You don't have to say anything, Mrs. Thurman. Just get inside where it's warm, and be thankful we were able to get through the fog."

"Speaking of the fog, it's getting thicker again," Wes said after they were in the Jeep. "Maybe we should head for Route 5 instead of following the river home. It will mean cutting over on Marshton Road, but we'll make better time."

Jennifer grimaced. "After what Willy and I went through last night, just thinking about Marshton Road gives me the jeebies, but I agree. We'll make better time, and I'm all for getting home just as quickly as possible."

They were on Marshton Road, with only a quarter of a mile to go before they reached the main highway, when the black truck popped up behind them. Jennifer let out a strangled cry. "It's the truck! No, don't turn around. Why is he doing this, Grandfather? Why?"

Wes jammed his hands in his coat pockets and muttered, "I have the feeling he's been following us from the time we lost him in the fog. Probably pulled off and waited for us to pass. I'll tell you what I'd like to do. I'd like to stop the Jeep and confront him!"

"But you know better, Grandfather. He

could have a weapon, or . . . Well, if it's Deke . . . The waitress at the bowling alley put it quite aptly. He's built like Godzilla, and I'd say she was being kind."

Wes grunted. "Okay. Let's look at this logically. Unless he tries to run us off the road, we have the protection of the Jeep. I say we head for town and see what happens."

"It'll be dark in another fifteen minutes, Grandfather."

Wes shrugged. "So we have lights, and he has lights. We can keep track of him that way, as long as the fog doesn't get worse and we end up in a ditch."

Jennifer had reached main highway, and turned right, praying the truck would turn left. It didn't, and she gritted her teeth. "What if he follows us all the way home? Maybe that's what he was trying to do last night."

"If he follows us into town, we'll head for the sheriff's house. Can't think of a better place for a showdown."

If we get to town, Jennifer thought, squinting her eyes as she tried to see through the fog. It was getting thicker, and the ensuing darkness was going to make it worse.

Wes said, "You're probably going to think I'm crazy, when we've got a maniac breathing down our necks, but all I can think about is a cup of hot coffee."

"We could stop at the bowling alley."

"Hmm—where we could also call the sheriff. Don't think I'd mind one bit if we were transported home in a patrol car."

"And what happens if the sheriff thinks we're nuts?"

"I'll talk to him this time, and I'll convince him we're not. You were with Willy last night, and now you're with me. We're in a different vehicle, and yet there he is, right on our bumper. If that doesn't open Jim's eyes, nothing will."

When they reached the bowling alley, Jennifer turned into the parking area and held her breath. When the black truck rolled on by, she let it out in one big swoosh.

Wes shook his head. "That doesn't mean a thing, Jennifer. I'm betting he'll park somewhere down the road, and wait. And then he'll be on our bumper again. Let's go in and make the call. I'm all for going home, but I'd like to get there alive."

Jennifer felt an ominous chill. Thinking along those lines was one thing, but hearing her grandfather put it into words was quite another.

Hand in hand, they walked into the nearly deserted building. Nobody was bowling, and the desk clerk wasn't 'Pete.' It was a different waitress too. Jennifer's heartbeat accelerated. If it was Tracy, maybe they could get some answers.

She pointed toward the bank of pay phones against the wall. "Why don't you make the call, Grandfather, while I get the coffee and talk to the waitress."

Wes fished in his pocket for a quarter. "Is that the waitress you talked to yesterday?"

"No, but maybe it's Tracy. Keep your fingers crossed."

"And say a little prayer," Wes muttered, heading for the phones.

Jennifer caught up with the pretty blond waitress as she was about to go into the kitchen, saw her name tag, and smiled. "Hi, Tracy. My name is Jennifer Gray. I talked to Penny yesterday."

The color drained from Tracy's face, and she shook her head. "I have nothing to say."

"Don't you think Roger needs the sheriff's help? Aren't you worried that he left the hospital that way, and hasn't been found? I know you're trying to protect him, but maybe he's in danger." Tracy clamped her mouth shut and Jennifer sighed. "Okay, have it your way. Could I just have two cups of coffee?"

Tracy whirled around and went into the kitchen, and Jennifer headed for the last table on the concourse. It was against the wall, in the shadows, and afforded her a panoramic view of the bowling alley, including the front door. Wes was making his way toward her, shaking his head.

"The sheriff is out working on a whole battery of calls," Wes said, sitting down across from her. "Nettie is ill, so a deputy is working dispatch. Poor guy is in a dither, but said he'd try to get through. Hope you had more luck with the waitress."

"I didn't. It's Tracy, but she won't talk to me. She's frightened, and I can understand that, but— Here she comes with our coffee."

Jennifer waited until Tracy had placed the coffee on the table before she said, "This is Wes Gray, Tracy. He's my grandfather, the pastor of the Calico Christian Church, and a very understanding man. He wants to help Roger too."

Tracy looked at Wes, and maybe it was

his kind face, but suddenly her eyes filled with tears. "Everything is such a mess . . . I told Roger he should go to the sheriff. What he did isn't so bad, but he's scared."

Jennifer took a deep breath. "Then I was right. You helped him get out of the hospital, and you're hiding him."

"Well, sort of. He feels so bad. I mean, physically. He keeps getting headaches, and he can't keep anything down . . ." She dropped to a chair. "I should be filling the salt shakers and the mustard jars . . ."

"Is your boss here tonight?"

She nodded. "He's in his office. He's been a good boss, but . . . I mean this bowling alley means everything to him, but . . ."

"But what, Tracy? Does Roger's problem have something to do with Jake Barnette?"

"Yes. It's so complicated, and scary. It's like a bunch of bowling pins. If one goes down, the rest will go down."

Wes said, "Why don't we tell you what we know, and then you can fill in the blank spots, Miss . . ."

"It's Quinn. Tracy Quinn."

"Then you're related to Tom Quinn at the Circle Q?"

"He's my uncle. If the boss comes out and sees me talking to you . . ."

"Does your boss know you've been dating Roger?" Jennifer asked.

"He knows. He saw us in Boodie's Roadhouse one night. We were trying to keep our relationship quiet, but that's pretty hard to do in a town this size."

"Were you trying to keep your relationship quiet because of Deke?" Wes asked.

Tracy's eyes opened wide. "You know about Deke?"

Jennifer said, "I talked to him last night, and Penny filled me in. Do you know if Deke drives a black truck?"

"A big black truck with a roll bar," Tracy said. "He's real proud of it, because he built it up from nothing into something."

"Is Deke one of those bowling pins you were talking about, that might take a fall?"

Tracy shook her head. "No. He likes me, that's all, and he hates Roger."

"Do you know anything about Deke?" Wes asked.

Tracy shrugged. "Not much. His name is Tony Dekesone, but everybody calls him Deke. He works as a ranch hand for my uncle, and he likes to bowl. Actually, he's the one who got me the job. He told me Mr. Barnette was looking for a waitress. I made the mistake of thanking him, and I guess he took it the wrong way. I tried to make him understand I was only interested in him as a friend, but he wouldn't give up."

"And then you met Roger."

"Yes, and Deke made our lives miserable. One time, we even saw him following us."

Jennifer shivered. "In his big black truck. Well, he's been following us around too, Tracy, and I'd sure like to know why."

Tracy frowned. "That's strange. Why would he want to follow you?"

"It started last night," Jennifer said. "I was here with a friend asking questions about Roger—"

"I know. Penny told me."

"—and when we left the bowling alley, Deke followed us. I won't go into the rest of it, but it was a harrowing experience, and then today, he followed us here. He drove on when we pulled into the bowling alley, but that doesn't mean he isn't out there somewhere, waiting."

Wes finished his coffee, and his brows furrowed together. "I gather you don't live on the ranch with your uncle?"

"No, I have my own apartment near the mall."

"And is that where you're hiding Roger?" Jennifer asked.

"No. We didn't think it would be safe. Mr. Barnette found us a little place that was empty and out of the way."

"Your boss? Maybe you'd better tell us how he fits in, Tracy."

Tracy wiped a hand over her eyes. "If I do . . ."

Wes said, "If you do, I have the feeling all those bowling pins you were talking about will come tumbling down. Was Roger responsible for putting the diamond necklace in our turkey?"

Tracy gasped. "*Your* turkey?"

"That's right, *our* turkey. Grandfather found the necklace when we were trying to get it defrosted. We turned it over to the sheriff, and he began the investigation. He came up with two possible suspects, and then narrowed it down to Roger after he disappeared from the hospital. We think the person who was supposed to get the diamond-stuffed turkey, didn't, and now he's after Roger."

Tracy sighed. "You're close, but that's all

I can say. You'll have to talk to Roger." She pulled a slip of paper off the order pad tucked in at her waist and wrote down the address. She handed it to Wes. "I know I shouldn't be doing this, but I'm so worried about Roger. The place only has a table, some chairs, and a cot, and it's so cold and drafty. He should be in the hospital."

"Did Roger say anything to you about the man who was supposed to pick up the turkey?"

"Yes . . . Look, I know you have to do what you have to do, but I only have a half hour left on my shift. If I can talk to Roger first, and try to explain . . ."

Wes shook his head. "I don't think that's a good idea, Miss Quinn. If he's frightened, and thinks you've betrayed him, he might run. And from what you've told us, he's in pretty bad shape. Let's try to get him back to the hospital first, and deal with the rest of it later."

Tears slipped down her cheeks. "Well, when you see him, tell him I love him . . ."

Tracy hurried away, and Jennifer felt her throat constrict. "We've put her in a terrible position, Grandfather."

"We didn't have much of a choice. I don't

know how Deke fits in, but I don't think he's the one we have to worry about. Go warm up the Jeep while I call dispatch. I'll give the address to the deputy so he can relay it to the sheriff, and then we're going home, with or without Deke on our bumper."

Jennifer looked at the address on the slip of paper. "It's one of those cottages on the corner of Marshton and River Road!"

Wes nodded. "Right under our noses all along."

Relieved to see the fog hadn't gotten worse, Jennifer was in the Jeep with the engine running when a short, thin man wearing a tan jacket hurried out of the bowling alley. His appearance didn't register at first, although something about him bothered her. And then she sucked in her breath. He fit the description of the stranger who had been in the market looking for Roger!

Wes walked out behind him, studying him thoughtfully, and climbed into the truck.

"That's him—the stranger from the butcher shop!" Jennifer practically yelped. "And that tells me Jake Barnette is right in the thick of it."

Bewildered by the turn of events, Jennifer watched the man get into a dark-colored sedan, and murmured, "What are we going to do?"

"Follow him. My guess is he's staying at the motel. Once we can establish that, we'll go on to the mall and call dispatch. Sooner or later the deputy will get through to the sheriff, and he's the one who has to handle it. I have a bad feeling about this, sweetheart. For one thing, there are too many players. He's turning right. Bet he's heading for the motel, all right."

Jennifer pulled out of the parking lot, and gripped the wheel. "He's going to see our lights, and know we're following him."

"Hmm, well, if he turns in at the motel, keep going."

"And if he doesn't? We can't . . . Oh, no!"

Wes turned around, stared at the headlights behind them, and muttered, "It has to be Deke."

Jennifer felt light-headed as she considered their predicament. "If Deke is working with the stranger, they've got us, Grandfather. We're sandwiched in, with no place to go!"

"We'll be coming up on Marshton Road in

about a minute, Jennifer. Make the turn without signaling, and let's see what happens. If Deke follows us, we can do the same thing you and Willy did last night, and head for the Cramer farm. I hate to put them at risk, but I don't see—"

Jennifer broke in with, "Look! The sedan is turning on Marshton Road!"

Before Wes could respond, the truck swept around and cut in front of them, nearly going into a slide in the process. By the time Jennifer had slowed down to make the turn safely, both vehicles had disappeared in the fog.

"Do you want to explain that to me?" she asked, trying to relax her grip on the wheel.

"I haven't a clue, unless Deke is after the stranger."

"Or they are on their way to see Roger. Birds of a feather. I know we should turn around and go home, but it wouldn't hurt to drive all the way to River Road, would it? I mean, if we see the truck and the sedan parked near the cottages, we'll have something important to report to the sheriff."

"Uh-huh, and those two men could be long gone before the sheriff ever gets wind of it."

"So what do you suggest we do?"

"You remember the old Cromwell sisters?"

"Of course I do. They were raised by their father and an uncle, and made moonshine. I remember the ruckus they caused the few times they came to church, because they smelled like liquor and fought during the service."

"Well, none of that has changed much, but they fell on hard times after their daddy and uncle died. Kept the old homestead going for a few years, and finally lost it to back taxes. They've been living in one of those cottages for the last three or four years. It's got low rent and it's away from the eyes of the town. Just the way they like it, but I don't imagine they would mind if we stopped in to use their phone if, in fact, we see the vehicles. After that, I suggest we watch and wait until help arrives."

Jennifer could hear the excitement in her grandfather's voice. "You're describing something very close to a stakeout, Grandfather."

"Just like in the movies."

"And what happens if the men take off before help arrives?"

"We'll leave that up to the sheriff."

"For somebody who wants to leave everything up to the sheriff, you're sure full of ideas."

Wes gave her a crooked grin. "As I see it, the sheriff can use all the help he can get, and you're not the only one in the family with a creative mind."

At the moment, Jennifer didn't feel creative at all, just frightened, and she prayed they were doing the right thing.

Chapter Eight

There was a community driveway between the two rustic cottages, with a parking area at the end. Lights were on in both houses, and smoke rose from the chimneys. It was calm and picture-perfect. Nothing seemed amiss except two familiar vehicles parked side-by-side.

Jennifer pulled the Jeep in behind the Cromwells' cottage and tried to gather her thoughts. She suddenly had the strange feeling nothing was as it seemed.

"I can hear the gears going around in your head," Wes said after a few moments. "You sense something odd too, don't you?"

"Yes, I do, and I think it has to do with seeing the truck and the sedan, parked like that. Cozy. Cordial. I can almost see the two drivers getting out, shaking hands, and walking into the cottage for a friendly meeting with Roger. They're all in it together, Grandfather, and that's what Tracy meant when she said it was like a bunch of bowling pins. If one goes down, they all go down."

"I take it you're including Jake Barnette in that?"

"Yes, and I think he's the boss, in more ways than one."

"The ringleader."

"I like your terminology. Have you been reading my mysteries too?"

Wes grinned. "So Jake is the ringleader, and Deke, the stranger, and Roger are all part of his gang. I'd say they're a bunch of jewel thieves, and Roger wasn't running from *them*. He was running from the law. They already knew that the Calico citizen who had found the necklace had turned it over to the sheriff, because that information was in the paper. But when the sheriff started poking around the bowling alley and asking questions, they felt the law closing in."

"Yes, but the sheriff didn't go to the bowling alley until after Roger disappeared. That's the part that doesn't make any sense. Wouldn't you think they would know Roger's disappearance would only create more questions, make Roger the prime suspect, and put the sheriff right in the thick of it?"

"You would think so, but maybe we're missing something. Shall we go inside before the Cromwell sisters call the cops on us? I saw one of them peeking out the window a few minutes ago, and it's hard to tell what they'll do."

Maybe they'd be greeted with shotguns, but Jennifer kept that thought to herself as they made their way around the house to the front porch.

Jennifer was thinking they still didn't have enough to pique the sheriff's interest, and that it would probably take a murder to bring him out this far on a night like this. Suddenly gunshots erupted from inside the cottage.

Wes had been about to knock on the door, and he froze with his arm still raised. Jennifer felt frozen too, in a paralyzing moment in time when danger felt as thick as the fog and all she could hear were the echoing shots and her pounding heart. And then the door opened. They could only stare at Frances Cromwell's angry face and at the shotgun pointed in their direction.

"Don't you move!" she commanded in one breath, and then, "Oh, my, we've made a terrible mistake, sister. It's the pastor and a pretty young lady!"

Fanny Cromwell pushed her glasses up on her nose, and peered over her sister's shoulder. Both women wore long, lace-trimmed black dresses and granny glasses, and had leathery skin. "Well, what on earth are you doin' out here in this weather, Pastor Gray? You came a cat's whisker away from gettin' your head blowed off!"

Frances scowled at her sister. "That's because you had the gun, and don't know one end from the other." She sighed. "Fanny blew a couple of holes in the ceiling the size of dinner plates before I could get it away from her. If I've told her once, I've told her a dozen times, if there is any shooting to do, let me handle it!"

Jennifer was aware that the three men across the road probably heard the shots too. Who knew what kind of a response it would bring? Not wanting to alarm the elderly women, Jennifer managed a smile and said, "We stopped by to wish you a happy holiday, and use your phone. I know you probably don't recognize me after so many years, but I'm Jennifer, the pastor's grand-daughter. If we can go inside . . ."

Frances shook her head in awe. "Little Jennifer Gray? My, oh my! Well, where's our hospitality on this cold, foggy night?" She placed the shotgun by the door, and stood aside. "Well, come in! Fanny was fixing a wassail bowl when you pulled up in back, and it should be about ready, unless it's floating with plaster. Well, we can just throw it out with the bath water, and start—"

Shots rang out again, interrupting Frances. And this time, they were coming from the cottage across the road.

While Frances and Fanny gasped and sputtered, Wes managed to get them into the living room. Jennifer closed the door.

"Sounds like somebody else is shooting holes in their ceiling," Wes said, looking around for the phone.

"If you're looking for the phone, it's right there beside my little reading chair," Frances said, brushing a wisp of gray hair out of her eyes. "My, oh my. I surely hope that nice young woman across the way isn't in trouble!"

"She isn't home," Fanny muttered. "Where's your head, sister? She drove off to work, remember? And you remember what I told you? I said I thought somethin' was fishy when that car and truck showed up." She looked up at Wes with a scowl on her weathered face. "Fishy, that's what it was. First one vehicle, and then the other. Two men. The first one walkin' into the cottage like he owned it, and the second one slinkin' around, peekin' through the windows. We tried to call the sheriff, but couldn't get through. Nothin' but static on the line. Gets that way sometimes after a storm."

' "Well, I have to give it a try," Wes said, dialing the sheriff's number. "You're right. I hear lots of static, but it's ringing . . ." And then his frown turned into a relieved smile. "It's Wes Gray again, Deputy. Have you managed to reach the sheriff? Good! You call him again, and tell him we're at the Cromwell sisters' cottage. Corner of River Road and Marshton. People are shooting guns, and we could have injuries. That's what I said, and tell him to hurry!"

Frances visibly relaxed. "Well, now that that's done, and we know that nice young woman can't be involved because she isn't home, and that nice sheriff is on his way, everything is fine and dandy. You can sit in front of the fire while you wait, and I'll see to the wassail. Might take some time if I have to start over."

Fanny straightened up the afghan on the ancient mohair sofa, and nodded. "Sit a spell and get warm while I slice some fruitcake. Made four of 'em last week, and some fruitcake cookies too."

After Fanny left the room, Wes said, "I'm so hungry, even fruitcake sounds good."

Jennifer sighed. "I don't know how you can be hungry at a time like this, Grandfather. There are three men over there, and we heard two shots. I don't want to even think about what that could mean."

"You know me well enough, Jennifer. When I feel stressed, I get hungry. Well, we have one consolation. We haven't heard the cars leave, so that means they are still there."

"But for how long? And don't forget, Tracy said she only had a half hour left on her shift. What if she walks into the middle of it?"

"Then best we watch for her, and head her off."

"If those men came here to kill Roger, then we're all vulnerable," Jennifer said with a shiver. "What's to stop them from coming over here and shooting us too?"

"Nothing, but they don't know we're here."

"No, but they know *somebody* lives here."

"Well, we're not defenseless," Wes said, nodding toward the shotgun. "And I have the feeling Frances is a crack shot."

"They must have heard the shots," Jennifer reasoned. "So they know there is a gun on the premises . . ."

"Well now, we are very lucky indeed," Frances said, carrying a tray into the living room. "Couldn't find one speck of plaster in the wassail, and Fanny's fruitcake sliced up just fine. Can't say much for the ceiling, though. I'll have to get somebody out here to fix it first thing in the morning, and hope it doesn't snow or rain in the meantime. Close the kitchen door behind you, Fanny. My, oh my, that kitchen will be cold in the morning. All that icy air coming in . . ."

"Won't stop me from fixin' tea and toast," Fanny announced. "Never was afraid of the cold. You're the one who walks around shiverin' all winter. Remember that time we had the busted window, and I woke up to a snowdrift in my bedroom? I just got the shovel and shoveled it out, while you groaned and moaned." She gave Wes and Jennifer a fetching smile. "I take after our daddy. *She* takes after our Uncle Mitford, who was never warm a day in his life. Help yourself to the wassail and fruitcake. If you'd come earlier, you could've shared a pot of soup. We eat early—a little after three, because it isn't good to go to bed on a full stomach. I got a book on the shelf that tells all about that."

While Fanny went on about the book, Jennifer tried to choke down a bit of fruitcake, and fought with a case of chills. She knew her grandfather was going to bolt for the door if he heard the sound of Tracy's car. But what if the men were out there, waiting? It was a terrifying thought, and kept her sitting on the edge of her seat.

"Jennifer?"

Jennifer blinked, and stared at her grandfather. "I'm sorry. Were you talking to me?"

"I said the fruitcake is mighty good, and you're going to have to get the recipe."

Jennifer groaned inwardly, and tried to swallow a sip of wassail. The fruitcake tasted like cheap brandy and candlewax, but the wassail was wonderful. Along with the roasted apples and spices it obviously contained a heavy mixture of ale and wine. Jennifer almost never drank, and on an empty stomach, it was going to go all the way to her toes, but she sipped it anyway. She noted that her grandfather did the same.

Wes looked at his watch and frowned. Jennifer knew he was concerned. The weather was foul, and Tracy was overdue.

Considering all the possibilities—that Tracy might have had to work late, or she might have driven her car into a ditch in the fog—Jennifer walked to the window and parted the brocade drapes. The fog was thicker, but she could still see the lights in the cottage across the road.

"No signs of life?" Wes asked, joining her at the window.

"No. Tracy should have been here by now."

"Maybe she decided to go home instead, so she wouldn't have to face the inevitable."

"You mean like the sheriff placing Roger under arrest, and hauling him off to jail? If it were only that simple."

When they returned to the sofa, their cups had been refilled with wassail, and two little boxes wrapped in red tissue paper were resting on the marred coffee table.

Frances chuckled. "See what happens when your back is turned? We decided to give you an early Christmas gift because you look so glum."

Fanny bobbed her head. "Somethin' to perk you up."

Jennifer flushed. "That wasn't necessary . . ."

Francis grinned. " 'Course it wasn't. But we did it anyway. Now you have to open your presents."

"Together now," Fanny said. "That way you'll see 'em at the same time."

Jennifer opened her box, and stared at the tiny shellacked wishbone tied with a bit of red ribbon.

Wes's wishbone was tied with green ribbon, and he held it up. "I have the feeling this holds some special significance," he said softly.

Fanny beamed. "It does. Every year, we roast two game hens for Thanksgiving. Tradition, you know. And every year we dry out the wishbones, shellack 'em, and put 'em on our Christmas tree. Means the following year will be full of good luck. Well, we decided to give 'em to you, 'cause you need good luck and cheering up."

"That was very sweet of you," Jennifer said.

Wes nodded. "That it was, and we'll follow your tradition, and put them on our tree. Thank you. Thank you both."

Fanny raised her cup of wassail. "To friendships that last through the ages—"

Her words were cut off by a pounding on the door. Jennifer looked at her grandfather and stiffened, but Frances and Fanny, who were totally unconcerned, beamed.

Before they could utter a word to stop her, Frances opened the door and exclaimed, "Well, this is certainly our night for company. I thought it might be the sheriff, but this is a pleasant surprise. Come on in, my dear, and sit by the fire. You look frozen clear through! Fanny, it's our new little neighbor from across the way. Get another cup of wassail!"

Tracy had been crying, but it only took Jennifer a moment to realize she had been crying with joy, not sorrow, because her face reflected a dozen emotions—happiness, elation, relief, and everything in between. And when she spoke, her words came out in an exuberant rush. "Pastor Gray . . . I-I just came over to use the phone, because . . . I'm so glad to see you! You have no idea what's happened! I was going to go home after work because I was afraid of what might be going on here, but then I got to thinking about Roger, and knew I couldn't let him face it alone. I expected to see the sheriff's car, but it wasn't here. Then I saw Deke's truck, and a dark sedan. I thought the sedan belonged to you, but the fact Deke was here worried me, so I parked down the road, and walked in. I don't know why I did that. Guess I thought if I had to get away in a hurry . . ."

Wes took Tracy by the arm and led her to the sofa. "Take a deep breath, Miss Quinn, and slow down."

"Sorry, but I feel like I'm about to explode! I have to call the sheriff . . ."

"The sheriff is on his way," Frances said,

handing Tracy a cup of wassail. "Drink this, and you'll feel better."

Tracy took a few swallows, but had to put the cup down because her hands were shaking. "This just proves what my father used to say. You don't really know somebody until there is a crisis. It's Deke. He's a hero! He saved Roger's life!"

"We heard two shots earlier," Jennifer said.

"That man's gun went off while he was struggling with Deke. Maybe you'd better come over to the cottage, and let Roger explain it. It's all so confusing!"

"Well, it's mighty exciting too," Fanny said, bobbing her head. "Bad men and good men, just like on TV."

A few minutes later, after instructing Frances and Fanny to stay put and wait for the sheriff, Jennifer and Wes followed Tracy across the road. They were completely confused. Deke was the hero, Roger was going to tell them all about it; but what about the stranger? Was he unconscious? Dead? Was this some kind of trap? The only thing that kept Jennifer going was Tracy's light, eager steps, and her own heartfelt prayers. Surely everything would be all right.

When they reached the door, Tracy opened it and stood aside. Wes went in first, and said, "Well, if this don't beat everything! Jennifer, look at this!"

The scene was easy to assess, and literally left Jennifer speechless. Roger and Deke were sitting at a little table, and the stranger was lying in the middle of the linoleum-covered floor, bound and gagged. Anger sparked in his dark eyes, but he couldn't do much more than struggle.

"Thought you two might be hanging around somewhere," Deke said, giving them a wide, toothy grin. "Where's the sheriff?"

"He's on his way," Tracy said, giving Roger a hug. "Do you feel up to telling them what happened?"

Roger, who would have been a nice-looking young man if he wasn't so battered and bruised, gingerly shook his head.

"I'll tell them," Deke said. "I've been followin' this little lady around for the last couple of days, so I would expect she needs to hear why, and why I had to do this my way."

Jennifer sat down on a rickety chair, and Wes stood behind her with a hand on her shoulder. She welcomed his strength and support, and muttered, "I'm all ears."

"I ain't very good at explaining things," Deke said, "so I'll make it easy on all of us, and say it in a few words. I knew Tracy was datin' Roger, here, and didn't like it. But I backed off because I know all about affairs of the heart. When it happens, you can't change it none, and it's stupid to try. But if you care about somebody, no matter how they feel about you, it's your place to protect 'em. I heard about old Roger disappearing from the hospital, and knew he was in trouble. Figured it had something to do with the boss man, 'cause I've seen them with their heads together, and figured the boss man was hiding old Roger from the law. Tracy didn't come to work the day Roger went into his vanishing act. Not the next couple of days, either, so I figured she was with him. Made me mad, 'cause that meant she could get into trouble too. Then the sheriff came to the bowling alley and started asking questions, then you, and that's when I had me a plan. Figured you'd find out where Roger was sooner or later, and if I followed you around long enough, you'd lead me right to him."

"What were you going to do after you found him?" Wes asked.

Deke puffed up his chest. "Call the sheriff and sit on him until the sheriff could haul him off to jail. But I got messed up last night. Thought you were leadin' me right to him until I saw the Cramer name on the mailbox. I know Mr. Cramer. He bought some hay from Mr. Quinn before the bad weather set in. Anyway, it was too late for me to drive on by, 'cause I'd already turned into the driveway. Didn't want to back up for fear I'd slide right off the road, so went all the way to the house, and turned around."

"And what about this afternoon?" Jennifer asked.

The grin widened. "You mean on River Road? That was luck, little lady. I was cruising around, hoping to spot Tracy's car, and then there you were. I knew it was you, 'cause I recognized the Jeep. Everybody in town knows the lady vet and her Jeep. I waited until you paid your little visit to that big house on River Road, and kept right on following you. When you stopped at the bowling alley, I moseyed on, turned around, and parked. But not before I seen the sedan in the parking lot. I knew it belonged to the creep." He pointed at the stranger. "He's been hanging around the bowling alley for the last couple of days, havin' lots of meetings with the boss man. When I seen you following him out of the bowling alley, I put it together. I decided he knew where old Roger was, you didn't, and that's why I had to follow him. When he turned in here, I kept going, and then doubled back, sneaky-like. I turned my lights off, and my motor, and just coasted right in beside his big fancy car. The lights inside was on, and I could see what was happening. He had a gun pointed at Roger, and that's when I rushed in. Seeing old Roger in jail is one thing, but I don't take kindly to murder."

Wes said, "And you struggled for the gun."

"Not at first." He nodded at the stranger. "He's little, but he's smart. He got the drop on me just as quick as you please. Wasn't until somebody started shootin' across the way that I could make my move. He took his eyes off me for a second, and I had him. He got off a couple of shots, but they went wild." He pointed at the far wall riddled with holes, and chuckled. "Now, I figure I got them both. The little guy is gonna go to jail for attempted murder, and old Roger for whatever. He won't say, but I'll bet he tells the sheriff."

Tracy looked at Roger. "Are you going to tell the sheriff?"

Roger took a deep breath. "I have to, Tracy. A jail cell would be better than this. Jake sent that man to kill me so I wouldn't talk. And there is something else you'd better know. You were on that man's hit list too, because you know about the necklace and Jake's past. Jake gave him instructions to kill us both. That wasn't why he came to Calico, but money is money. A payoff for two murders would be better than leaving town empty-handed."

"Then if Deke hadn't gotten here when he did . . ."

"We'd both be dead."

Deke's cheeks puffed up, and his face grew dark with anger. "I shoulda killed him."

"And then you would be going to jail too," Wes reasoned. He looked at Roger. "We know you put the necklace in the turkey, Roger. Was that man supposed to get it? Orris said he came into the market looking for you the day of the accident."

Roger sighed, and every breath he took

was an effort. "I was a clerk in Jake Barnette's western boot shop in Lincoln. I found out he was using the shop as a cover to fence stolen jewelry, but I never said anything because I wanted to keep my job. Then Jake told me he was moving to Calico, and was going to build a bowling alley. I stayed on in Lincoln with the new owner of the boot shop, and I'd probably still be there if that man hadn't come in one day, asking for Jake. He was carrying a boot box, and looked real nervous. The owner wasn't there, and I was about to tell him Jake had retired, when he saw a cop car cruise by. He dumped the box on the counter, and took off. I knew something amazing must have been in the box even before I looked. The diamond necklace was inside one of the boots. I had two choices then. Call the cops, or keep the necklace. Problem was, what was I going to do with a stolen necklace? I was renting a room a couple of blocks away, and that night, I took the necklace home. I figured sooner or later, the guy would come back for it, and solve my problems. But he didn't.

"Two weeks later, I packed up everything I owned in my car, and headed for Calico. I figured Jake would know what to do with the necklace. To make a long story short, he was really mad. Said he'd left that kind of life behind. He was a respectable citizen now, and wanted to keep it that way. But I guess he felt sorry for me too, because I'd given up everything to make the move, and I was broke. He also said I reminded him of himself when he was young—eager, but without brains. He helped me get a place to stay, and found me a job at the butcher shop. He told me I had to keep the necklace with me, because he didn't want any part of it, but that he'd put out some feelers. He said it might take time, because a lot of the men he'd worked with were out of the business too. Meanwhile, I met Tracy, and we fell in love . . ."

Roger was in physical distress, perspiring heavily, and taking deep, ragged breaths. There was a cot in the corner of the sparsely furnished room, but when Jennifer suggested he lie down, he refused. "Th-this needs to be told," he muttered.

Wes spoke up. "Then let me fill in the rest. You can stop me if I get something wrong. Jake finally found a contact, and the contact was supposed to pick up the necklace from you on the Tuesday before Thanksgiving.

Only you had to deliver a turkey to the But-ler farm, and got into an accident on the way back to town. You were in the hospital when the man came into the shop looking for you. So much for the necklace that was stuffed in one of the turkeys. You were the only one who knew which turkey it was, and you were in the hospital."

Roger leaned his head against Tracy and closed his eyes. "It wasn't supposed to be in a turkey. I was given the guy's description. He was supposed to come in on Tuesday, and ask me for a fresh capon. I had the neck-lace in my apron pocket, already wrapped in butcher paper. All I had to do was stuff it in the capon, and give it to the guy."

"How were you supposed to get the money?" Wes asked.

"After he had the necklace, he was sup-posed to put the money under the front seat of my car. It was in the parking lot, un-locked. But things were a little crazy that day. The fresh turkeys from North Platte were delivered, for one thing, and they had to be counted and logged in. And Orris was in a bad mood, ordering me to do this and do that. He knew I was nervous. Probably thought it was because he was yelling at me, but that wasn't it. I kept waiting for something to go wrong. I had a stolen necklace in my pocket, and it was making me nuts. When I saw a deputy heading for the meat counter, I scooted into the back room and shoved the necklace in a fresh turkey. Took me only a second to wrap it up and toss it in the back of the freezer. What happened after that seems like a crazy comedy or something."

Wes nodded. "You realized the deputy wasn't after you, Orris told you to deliver a turkey to the Butler farm, and you had to leave the necklace in the turkey."

"Yeah, because I didn't have time to get it out. I took Orris's truck because my car is a chuggedy piece of junk, and I wanted to get there, and get back quick. I figured if the guy came in while I was gone, Orris would tell him I was making a delivery, and he'd wait. I was going too fast along a bad stretch of road, and had the accident. As soon as I could, I called Jake from the hospital. I think that was the next day. And I'll never forget his words: 'Well, by the time the contact is finished with you, you'll probably wish you'd died in that accident, Roger, because men like that don't take kindly to screw-ups. He came a long way to get that necklace, and now he's going home empty-handed. If I were you, I'd sleep with my eyes open.' I got scared, especially when I remembered the tough-looking men coming and going from the boot shop all the time, and that's when I called Tracy. I told her everything. When I told Jake I'd told her everything, that's when he said he had a place for me to hide, if Tracy could help get me out of the hospital."

Jennifer said, "Then it was a setup."

Roger nodded. "I think Jake was wrestling with his conscience. That's the only reason he didn't have me killed sooner. But he couldn't leave any loose ends, either."

"Like me," Tracy said, shivering.

Jennifer heard the sirens approaching, and sighed with relief. The nightmare was finally over.

Within minutes, the Cromwell sisters had escorted the sheriff and two deputies into the cottage, and the women didn't look the least bit surprised to see the man on the floor. Frances, who was carrying the shotgun, waved it at Deke. "And that's the other one, Sheriff. That's the man we saw sneaking around. Arrest him too!"

The sheriff holstered his gun, and sighed. "I appreciate all your help, Frances, but I think it would be best if you take Fanny and your shotgun home, and let me handle this. This is police business, and . . ."

Frances planted her feet. "We're not budging one inch, sheriff. All you've got are those little pea-shooter guns. You need my shotgun, and my good aim. Don't worry. I got 'em covered."

Fanny nodded. "You arrest the outlaws, and then we'll all have some fruitcake and wassail."

"There is only one outlaw here," Wes said, pointing at the stranger. "And he isn't going anywhere."

Roger spoke up. "Make that two outlaws, sheriff. I'm ready to make a full statement."

"The statement can wait until we get you to town where we can do it properly," the sheriff said.

"It can't wait," Roger insisted. "If Jake hears about this before you can pick him up, he'll run, and then nobody will be safe."

"Jake. Jake Barnette?"

Wes spoke up. "It's a long story, Jim, and Barnette is right in the middle of it. He hired the man on the floor to kill Roger and Tracy."

"Go pick up Barnette," the sheriff said to his deputies, "and take him to my office. We're gonna straighten this out in town, where we can all be warm and comfortable." He gave Jennifer and Wes a wan smile. "You two okay?"

"We're fine," Wes said. "By the way, Deke is the hero in this, so go easy on him." He gave Jennifer a hug. "Let's go home, sweetheart. It's been a long day, and we still have to call Emma."

Jennifer groaned. "Emma is going to think we've dropped off the face of the earth."

Frances clucked her tongue. "Nobody is going anywhere until we package up some fruitcake for you all to take along. Looks like everybody needs some cheering up to me!"

"How about if we let the sheriff get on with his work, Frances," Wes said pleasantly. "Jennifer and I can take the fruitcake to town and see that everybody gets their share."

"Hmm, well, I suppose that would be okay. What do you think, Fanny?"

Fanny frowned in thought. "We should

send along some wassail too, sister. Now, if I can just remember where I put that big old milkin' bucket with the lid . . ."

Jennifer grinned and took her grandfather's hand. It was going to be a long night, in more ways than one.

"I look a fright!" Emma exclaimed, trying to pat down her unruly brown hair. "I swear the hospital shampoo isn't fit for man or beast, and my skin is so dry it crackles like leaves in the fall. Static electricity too. Everything I touch goes 'zap,' and I know I've gained five pounds just lying here. Soup, rice, and Jell-O, that's all they know how to fix. I kept telling them to give me salads and vegetables, but they wouldn't listen."

Emma was wearing her new flowered dress, and looked much healthier. Her cheeks were flushed with excitement, and her eyes were as bright as the blue sky.

Wes took his eyes off the road for a moment and gave Emma a winsome smile. "That sounds better than the fruitcake Jennifer and I have been eating for the last two days, though I have to admit it isn't bad."

Emma grunted. "You never did tell me why you were visiting the nutty Cromwell sisters. But I put it together after I read John, Jr.,'s story in the paper. Can't fool me. You were right in the middle of that mess. I figure you'll tell me how and why sooner or later, and I can wait. Well, will you just look at the town! It's all dressed up for Christmas. The lights are up, windows are all decorated red and green, and the streets are full of shoppers. Seems like I've been in the hospital for months instead of only a few days. Was I ever relieved to see blue sky this morning. Couldn't stand one more day of fog. Did you pack my new slippers, Jennifer?"

Jennifer leaned over from the back seat and kissed Emma's cheek. "I packed your new slippers, and the trunk is stuffed with your gifts."

"Well, I'm glad we decided to have the flowers and plants distributed around the hospital. Where's my bear?"

"In the trunk."

"Hmm. I talked to Nettie yesterday, and she's feeling better. She said it's a good thing, because the sheriff is in a muddle. With that bowling alley man and his friend in jail waiting arraignment, and Roger under guard at the hospital, he has enough to keep him busy until the new year. Guess Ida isn't happy about that."

"Well, he doesn't have to worry about Roger," Jennifer said. "He won't run again. He wants to face this, and get on with his life. I don't know how it's going to turn out, but about all they have him on is receiving stolen goods, and even that part of it is confusing, because Roger wasn't the intended receiver. And he's never been in trouble before. Willy thinks he'll get off. But no matter what happens, Tracy will be waiting for him."

"And what about that man named Deke?"

"It turns out that he's a gentle giant whose only crime was to try to protect Tracy. He didn't go about it the right way, but nobody can fault him for that. A lot of people in town think he's a hero, and in a way, I guess he is."

Emma chuckled. "And most of the folks in town are still trying to figure out who got the turkey with the diamond necklace. Maybe one of these days we should tell 'em, and put their minds to rest. Oh, look, I can see the steeple. We're almost home!"

"Home," Jennifer said. "And now that

you're back, Emma, we can begin the Christmas season together, like a family."

"Amen," Wes said, with a tremor in his voice.

Emma didn't comment, but reached over and patted his hand. It was a simple gesture, but it was worth a thousand words.